FRONTIER'S CALLING

FRONTIERS BOOK 2

ROBERT C. JAMES

Copyright © 2021 by Robert C. James

All rights reserved.

No part of this book may be reproduced in any form or by any electronic or mechanical means, including information storage and retrieval systems, without written permission from the author, except for the use of brief quotations in a book review.

All characters and events in this publication, other than those clearly in the public domain, are fictitious and any resemblance to real persons, living or dead, is purely coincidental.

Cover design by Yvonne Less, Art 4 Artists

ONE

Caput Mundi House - Istanbul, Earth

"I won them the war, and this is how they repay me?"

President Glendon Jarret clenched his jaw and slammed his fist against his desk. "Where are the polls at their worst?"

His media advisor, Patrick Ryland, checked his data tablet. "Your numbers continue to struggle on Centauri. But that's not unexpected."

"Naturally," Glendon lamented. "I shouldn't have agreed to give those people back the vote after the war."

"Your popularity has also fallen across the outer worlds," Ryland continued. "Our polling in those population centers reveal heightening Marauder attacks, and your speech last month against their plans for independence as major concerns."

"What about Earth?"

"Support is slipping further. There are areas where

you're still favored, but it's been dwindling every year you've been in office."

It had been universally agreed that if he hadn't been elected during the Earth-Centauri War, it would have waged much longer than it had. More people would be dead and the conflict may have even been lost. Glendon couldn't live with the embarrassment of being thrown out after one term. "I've heard enough. Send in Ntini."

Ryland nodded and exited, while Glendon stood and walked over to the window, taking in the vast skyscrapers of Istanbul. The gorgeous old-world architecture complemented the modern metropolis, creating one of the most breathtaking vistas on the planet.

Napoleon Bonaparte once remarked that if Earth ever had one true capital city, it should be Constantinople, where east meets west. When the commonwealth was formed, the founders had taken his advice. Glendon often thought about the emperors of the ancient town and wondered if any of them could've imagined that one day the fate of not only Earth, but many other worlds, would be decided on the same patch of dirt, where they once stood.

The door to the office opened, and Luan Ntini stepped in. "Mister President."

Glendon turned to his chief of staff, who ambled to the front of the desk with his hands behind his back. "You've looked at the polls?"

Luan nodded. "This morning."

"I'm in trouble."

"As with all opinion polls from the *Martian*

Tribune, we must be wary of how often they swing."

"You know as well as I, even if it's a slight outlier, all the other polls confirm they're in the same ballpark." Glendon sat behind his desk. "Our internal surveys show similar problems throughout the commonwealth."

Luan sat across from him. The sage old man had been the president's confidant since he'd taken office and was the rock of his administration.

"If things stay as they are," Glendon continued, "I will lose the election in a year's time."

"I won't lie—"

"Good, because I don't pay you to."

"If we follow the trajectory we're on now, not only are you going to lose but you'll face a wipeout like no other president has since the founding of the United Earth Commonwealth."

Glendon narrowed his eyes at the portraits of the various presidents on the wall who had come before him, wondering how loyal the people were to them. "I was their savior."

"To be blunt, Mister President, the public don't care. You were who they needed in wartime. Now they want a leader during the peace." Luan steepled his fingers. "The British hailed Winston Churchill in a similar light during World War II. But that didn't stop his soldiers returning home and voting him out of office. And he didn't have to contend with…"

Glendon glared at his as chief of staff, as he trailed off mid-sentence. "You were saying?"

Luan cleared his throat. "He didn't have to contend

with concerted opposition objecting to his use of tritonium weapons ending the war."

"See, that's what I pay you for." Glendon stood and paced behind his desk. He pondered about the main issue he'd had since the end of the rebellion. By forcing its conclusion with tritonium weapons, not only were pacifists protesting against him, he had an opposition leader in the parliament constantly calling him a war criminal. "Well, we know what the problem is, what do we do about it?"

Luan's eyes betrayed a man who'd had restless nights thinking of just that. "Win Earth and win the presidency. If we can gain back the swings here, it won't matter how the rest of the commonwealth votes."

"Any ideas?"

Luan opened his mouth, but before he could say anything, Glendon's secretary's voice rang out over the intercom.

"Mister President, the Minister of Defense is here to see you."

"Send him in."

The door to the office once again swung ajar, and Minister Takashi strode in. "Mister President," he greeted his superior.

Glendon put a hand out to take a seat next to Luan. "What brings you here today? I thought you were in Miami."

"It's actually Miami that brings me here, Mister President."

"Oh?"

"Do you remember the briefing I gave you on the Orion V incident?"

"How could I forget?" The mystery of what had happened at the far-flung mining operation had been foremost on Glendon's mind ever since he'd received word of its destruction. The fleet carrier, *Repulse*, which he'd sent out, had found few answers. If anything, they'd discovered more mysteries with the *Vanguard*'s debris in orbit. Analysts assumed someone found out about the discovery of the ancient extraterrestrial artifact beneath the planet's surface, and possibly of the extraterrestrial the *Vanguard* was transporting there.

Glendon wanted answers before anything hit the presses. If his presidency wasn't already in trouble, it would be with the death of over a thousand people near the Reach.

"Do you remember me mentioning the *Argo*?" Takashi asked.

"The cargo ship that logged a flight plan to Frontier's Reach from Vesta III?"

None of the analysts believed the *Argo* responsible for what happened at Orion V. It was more likely they were responding to a distress call, as their buyer from Tau-Zeta claimed.

"Well, Mister President," Takashi said, excitedly, "the *Argo* has miraculously appeared, and they're heading for Outpost Watchtower as we speak."

Glendon raised an eyebrow. "Has there been any communications broadcast by the *Argo*?"

"Only that they've got damage and an injured

Doctor Susan Tai on board."

"Susan Tai? The doctor from TIAS?"

Takashi nodded.

"Which confirms the *Argo* was at Orion V. They could know a great deal. Is the *Repulse* nearby?" Glendon asked.

"It is."

"Good. Make arrangements with Admiral Mueller to intercept the *Argo*. They mustn't reach Outpost Watchtower. Also ensure any further communications are jammed."

"Yes, Mister President."

Glendon peered across at Luan, pondering before returning his attention to his Minister of Defense. "Do we happen to have any Zero-Five operatives in the area?"

Takashi fidgeted in his seat. "We do."

While Glendon was reticent to use them, their skills could come in handy. "Liaise with the Minister of Intelligence and put them on standby."

"Yes, Mister President."

"Okay, that'll be all."

Takashi stood and left the office, closing the door behind him.

"Do you think Zero-Five will be really necessary?" Luan asked.

"It's best to plan for all contingencies, just in case..." Glendon shrugged. "Now, where were we? That's right. You were going to tell me how to win next year's election."

TWO

Cargo Ship Argo

"Unable to achieve commlink."

Jason Cassidy shook his head at the computer's confirmation. After contacting Outpost Watchtower and apprising them of the *Argo's* situation, all communications in the area had been jammed. He wasn't surprised. He knew how the military worked.

Jason sat back recalling the success of the *Argo's* return trip through trans-space. Just as last time, the crew were all knocked out from the effects of the trans-space corridor and awoke upon the ship's departure from the vortex. What had been unusual was they hadn't exited at Orion V where Professor Petit had expected. He'd theorized it was because the corridor had decayed since their first journey through it. Luckily, however, it put them half a light-year closer to Outpost Watchtower where they were heading for the aid they desperately sought.

Jason turned back to the console and ran his hands over the keypad. The comms may have been jammed, but he still had a few tricks up his sleeve from his days in the service.

"Data packet sent."

He smiled and stood, walking from the bridge, leaving the autopilot to do its thing. In the A Deck corridor, he bumped into the hulking figure of Conrad Althaus.

The man was a wreck. He'd taken Tyler's passing worse than anyone else, which was saying something considering how sick Jason felt. The pair stared at each other, but neither had anything to say. Althaus simply brushed by him and walked through the hatchway onto the bridge.

Past the elevator shaft, Jason entered the engine room. Spare parts had been scattered everywhere. Since they'd exited the trans-space corridor, it'd been all hands on deck to repair the small cargo ship, and as usual, chaos was the norm before anything could return to the way it was. He poked his head around, wondering where everyone was. A clang sounded from one of the maintenance junctions, and Aly slid out, looking grimier than usual.

"How's it coming?" Jason asked.

"Getting there slowly." Aly threw down a set of fried linkages on the maintenance console.

"Where's Professor Petit? I thought he was helping you."

"He was, but Doctor Tai was waking up for the day, and I said he should go and see her."

"That's fair." Jason's looked around the engine room and his mind wandered.

"Are you okay?"

He was far from it, but he didn't want it to show. During his time in the service, every leader he'd served under kept their emotions in check no matter the situation. They always appeared as if they were in control. He had to do his best to emulate them, especially with the crew now relying on him to get them home. What he'd do after that, however, was something else entirely. As long as he was far away from the *Argo*, he didn't really care.

"I'm fine."

She looked at him knowingly. "Uh-huh?"

"Keep me updated with your progress."

Aly nodded, and Jason strolled from the engine room and turned into the infirmary. He peered through the observation screen at Doctor Susan Tai lying in her bed with Petit and Kione sitting beside her. The tired figure of Kevin Rycroft appeared alongside him. Jason couldn't help but notice the youthful glint in his eyes all but dulled.

"How's our patient?" he asked the makeshift doctor.

"She's not getting any better." Kevin rubbed his hands over his eyes. "If we don't get her to a proper medical facility soon, she'll die."

Enough people have died out here.

"What about Kione? Has he exhibited any of those mental powers since leaving the weapon ship?"

"It doesn't appear so. Whatever connection he had with the sphere is gone, along with any of his abilities." Kevin leaned on the door, almost slipping down it. "How long until we reach Outpost Watchtower?"

"Two days. Will she hold on?"

"I believe so. Do you think we'll make the outpost?"

It was a question Jason had wondered himself since the comms had been jammed. "I hope so."

"If you need me, I'll be in the galley getting a coffee." Kevin put a reassuring hand on his shoulder, and disappeared into the outer corridor.

Jason nudged the door open to the infirmary where Tai was sleeping. Over the speakers, a piece of classical music played. Its soothing sound echoed off the bulkheads. He stared at Kione in the bed opposite her. It was hard to take his eyes off him. Even after all they'd been through, the extraterrestrial still astonished him. He was a far cry from the aliens in *The Bug People of Alpha Prime*, but nonetheless their he lay.

Petit stood from Tai's bedside. "Mister Cassidy, I hope you don't mind me leaving the engine room for—"

"Please, we appreciate all the help you've given us. I know you and Doctor Tai are friends." He pointed up to the speakers. "What's this?"

"*Ode to Joy*. Beethoven."

"Not many people are into the classics these days."

"She said Captain Marquez played it once. I guess she finds it comforting."

"Bridge to Jason," Althaus hailed him over the intercom.

"Go ahead," Jason said, pulling his commband toward his mouth.

"The scanners have picked up a bogey heading our way. It's a commonwealth carrier."

Jason's stomach clenched and he turned to Petit. "It would seem they've sent in the big guns."

The giant CDF ship heaved out of FTL and approached the *Argo*, her immense size filling the bridge's viewport. During the war, whenever Jason saw a carrier it was a joyous sight. Now it just made him nervous.

"I'm detecting a pair of fighters heading our way," Althaus said from the operations station.

The two craft emerged from the stern of the huge vessel and veered toward the *Argo* on an intercept course.

"They're opening a commlink," his uncle informed him.

Jason took a seat in the captain's chair. "Let's hear it."

"Cargo Ship Argo, *this is Admiral Kostecki of the fleet carrier* Repulse. *Deactivate your engines and go to maneuvering thrusters. Our fighters will escort you to our hangar deck. On arrival, prepare for boarding."*

Jason never much liked being told what to do. "This is—"

"The commlink's been cut off," Althaus said.

"Sons of bitches hung up on me!"

Aly and Kevin appeared from the hatchway, and made their way to their stations.

"I suppose we've got no choice." Jason placed a hand on Kevin's shoulder at the helm. "Do as they've instructed. Let them show us the way in."

Within moments, the darkness of space disappeared, and the *Argo* found itself in the new surroundings of the *Repulse's* hangar deck. With a thud, Kevin brought the old girl down and the hangar deck pressurized around them. A team of Marines burst out from the interior door of the *Repulse* and bounded toward the *Argo*.

"Open the rear access ramp," Jason said.

Althaus stared at him for a moment, then relented. He knew as well as Jason they'd come aboard regardless. No one wanted to see explosives being used. The ramp came down, and the Marines stepped on board. A few minutes later, they appeared on the bridge.

Jason took a seat in the captain's chair swiveled around to face them. From behind the Marines, a woman with commander rank pins on her collar strode toward him.

"Tyler Cassidy?"

Jason twitched at his brother's name. He remained in his seat and crossed his arms. A hush permeated around the bridge.

"Jason Cassidy, actually," he said.

"Jason? Our files—"

"Are out of date. Tyler died responding to a CDF distress call."

"I'm sorry to hear that. You understand we're all here because of what happened at Orion V."

"Obviously." Jason stared back at her. "The stompers are a bit much, aren't they?"

She turned to the Marines and they promptly departed through the hatchway. "I'm Commander Hariri. I'll be overseeing your debriefings."

She put out a hand.

Jason shook it under sufferance. "I guess we have little choice in the matter."

"You do not."

At least she's honest.

"Doctor Tai is in our infirmary," Jason said. "She's—"

"Already being taken to the sickbay aboard the *Repulse*. She'll then be transferred to Outpost Watchtower when we arrive."

"The *Argo*—"

"Will be repaired, so that after your debriefings you'll be able to go on your way without inconvenience."

"And my people?"

"Will be treated as guests on the *Repulse* while you're here." She peered around the bridge. "Does that satisfy all your inquiries?"

While Jason could never be completely content, it would do for the moment. He was surprised they were being so accommodating. "Let's get this over with."

Aly walked up beside him and clutched his hand.

Jason squeezed back and looked into her eyes. "Just answer all their questions truthfully. The sooner we're done, the sooner we'll get out of here."

I hope...

THREE

UECS Repulse

Javier couldn't take his eyes off the paraphernalia in Admiral Kostecki's office. Medals, guns, and hunting trophies adorned every square inch of bulkhead. It was the home of a man of war.

"Professor Petit, please sit down."

Javier took a chair on the opposite side of the desk, while the admiral studied a data tablet, creating an awkward silence.

"I've been reading over the report you submitted to Commander Hariri." Kostecki put the tablet down. "I must say, you've had quite the adventure."

"I would hardly call what we went through an adventure," Javier bristled.

"No. The losses on Orion V and the crew of the *Vanguard*..." He tapped his fingers on the desk. "Captain Marquez is a great loss. And these Seekers...a scary proposition to say the least. What's most disturbing is we don't truly know who they are. In your report you state they were using the native inhabitants of Psi-Aion as slaves."

"And Christian Nash as well."

"You couldn't determine how they were controlling these individuals?"

"No."

"Do you believe we've got further cause for concern?"

"Admiral?"

"You destroyed their super weapon and one of their ships. In your report, the Seekers sent a message to a distant star system before their destruction. Might they come searching for redemption?"

"That's something only the Seekers can answer." Though it was a question Javier had asked himself as well. "But from everything we saw, they viewed us as a lower life-form. They—"

"A lower life-form that threw a spanner in their works," Kostecki said. "This trans-space technology they wield. Should they want to take revenge…"

"As I said, Admiral, that's not a question I can answer."

"Hmm." Kostecki glanced back at the tablet. "Speaking of the transient space method that you replicated. Could it be done again?"

"I was working with an already created aperture," Javier told him. "By using the Iota particles I'd salvaged from our first journey, I was able to reopen it for the return trip."

"And creating one from scratch would be more difficult?"

"A technological impossibility, at least for now."

Kostecki stared at him with unwavering eyes. "Moving on to Kione. Your theory regarding his connection to the sphere is a little murky."

"Theories tend to be that way."

"But you believe his people created the sphere?"

"Since it was his genetic code that opened it, I would assume it likely."

"But this artifact is six million years old."

"That doesn't mean his species don't still exist." Javier peered around the room at the trophies Kostecki had collected on safari and wondered how many of them would be around in six million years.

"Do you believe he's a Seeker?"

Javier smiled. "Since we don't know what a Seeker looks like, that's difficult to determine. However, by the way Christian Nash regarded him, I would assume it unlikely."

"Regardless, it's unsettling to think of the power his people are capable of, not to mention the mental abilities he wielded when he was in contact with the sphere."

"Those abilities have since disappeared with the sphere's destruction."

"For now..."

"Yes, well, once we reach Watchtower and they can treat Doctor Tai, she'll be able to determine for sure—"

"No doubt. All right, this seems to be all for now.

I'm sure as the debriefings of the *Argo* crew get underway, I'll have more questions that will need answering." Kostecki placed the data tablet in front of Javier. "Please read this carefully."

Javier inspected the nondisclosure agreement. By signing, it bound him to absolute secrecy in regards to everything that had happened from the attack on Orion V to the moment he'd walked into Kostecki's office. He'd signed many throughout his career. He placed his thumbprint on the data tablet and slid it back over to the admiral. "What about the crew of the *Argo*?"

"They'll be debriefed as you've been. I'll collate all information so we can have an accurate picture of what happened." Kostecki rose from his chair. "Now, the *Repulse* will arrive at Outpost Watchtower in the next few hours. You're welcome to go aboard the station. After I conclude the debriefs, we'll be returning to Earth so we can take you back to TIAS."

"And Doctor Tai?"

"If she's well enough to travel, she'll come with us."

Javier nodded his appreciation and walked from the office. His thoughts returned to Jason Cassidy and his crew. He hoped their debriefs went as smoothly as his own.

Outpost Watchtower

Commander David Ortega gazed through the large viewport in the operations center. In the distance, the *Repulse* grew steadily bigger as it approached.

"Commander, the *Repulse*'s opening a commlink," Ensign Brock, the station's communications officer, informed him from the other side of the operations center.

"Let's hear it," David said.

"Repulse to Outpost Watchtower, requesting clearance to enter security perimeter."

David perused the exit and entry lanes surrounding the station. He knew they were clear, but for safety purposes he had to be absolutely sure.

"Clearance is granted, *Repulse*," he said. "Our medical team will stand by for Doctor Tai's arrival."

"Affirmative Watchtower. Repulse out."

"Instruct Doctor Lenard to proceed to the hangar deck."

Brock nodded and did as instructed, while David made his way into the central elevator shaft of the space station. He wondered about Jason Cassidy. He'd got himself caught up in something that was being kept very quiet. Even Watchtower's CO hadn't been told about it. He could only assume it had something to do with the attack on Orion V.

The elevator doors opened, and Doctor Lenard appeared along with her medical team and a mobile stretcher bed.

"Have the doctors from the *Repulse* sent all the information you require?" he asked her, stepping in beside her.

The doors to the elevator closed, and they were back on their way.

"Yes, they have," she said.

He expected her to elaborate, but she said no more. David found it odd, but considering the top-secret nature of everything, he wasn't surprised.

The elevator came to a halt at the top deck of the space station, and the transport pod from the *Repulse* made its final approach. The large hangar doors closed behind it. As it safely landed at the center of the bay, the deck pressurized, and Lenard and her team got the green light to exit the viewing gallery.

Doctor Tai came out of the rear airlock of the transport pod with the *Repulse's* medical team, and Lenard exchanged pleasantries with her opposite number. As the doctor led her team through the viewing gallery, David got a look at the prone body of Tai on the medical stretcher. A pang of guilt had festered away in the pit of his stomach ever since he'd received the first transmission from the *Argo*. He knew if it wasn't for him giving Jason the data regarding the Iota particles, he wouldn't have got embroiled in this mess.

FOUR

UECS Repulse

Jason paced around the small set of quarters, admiring his surroundings. They were pleasant and much more spacious than anything he'd had when he'd been assigned aboard the *Raptor*. He would have loved to serve on a fleet carrier during the war. But even with the soft lighting and modern décor, it was just an elaborate cage. The door was locked from the outside, and a pair of Marines stood guard in the corridor. He thought of the others and hoped they were being treated well.

He picked up a piece of chocolate on the counter of his kitchenette and unwrapped it as a knock came from the door. It opened and one of the guards stepped in.

"Commander Hariri will see you now," the gruff stomper said.

Jason broke a chunk of chocolate off and followed the Marine out. The other wide-shouldered soldier escorted him to his destination and ushered him through a door and into another room. It was bright but spartan, except for a table sitting in the center with a chair on each side. Jason chuckled to himself. It may not have been dark, and there was no light dangling from the ceiling, but he knew an interrogation chamber when he saw one.

The door behind him opened, and Commander Hariri walked in with a case in her hand. She strode past him and sat on the chair on the opposite side of the table. "Take a seat, please, Mister Cassidy," she said.

He eyed her warily and got comfortable. She put the case on the table and pulled a pair of data tablets from it, sliding one over to him.

"Please place your thumbprint on there and state your full name for the record."

He did as instructed. "Jason Benjamin Cassidy."

"Thank you." She took the tablet and looked it over, no doubt confirming the details. She then placed it back in her case. "Now, before we begin, I'd like to make you aware that I'll be recording this debriefing. All questions asked must be answered truthfully." She pointed to a red light emanating from the bulkhead behind him. "If you don't, I'll know about it."

Jason glanced at the PLD-4000. It could read his speech, body language, facial features, perspiration, and skin alterations. A foolproof piece of military and intelligence hardware.

"Are you ready to begin?" she asked.

Jason nodded.

"Excellent." She put her hands on the table. "Your

flight manifest has you listed as a passenger. When the *Repulse* found you, it was assumed you were the *Argo's* commanding officer."

"My brother, Tyler Cassidy, was owner and captain of the *Argo*. I'm taking over temporarily."

"According to our discussion aboard your ship earlier, you claim he was lost along with Captain Marquez when they attempted to escape the Seeker weapon ship's destruction."

A lump formed in Jason's throat. "Correct."

"I'm sorry, Mister Cassidy." Hariri appeared genuinely saddened. "Can I ask why you were a passenger aboard the *Argo*?"

"I'd booked passage to Frontier's Reach."

"For what purpose?"

"I was searching for a clue to the death of Christian Nash."

"Yes, I read the *Raptor's* mission report, regarding the Nebula TPA-338 incident. A lot of good people died that day, including Lieutenant Nash." Her eyes narrowed. "Why Frontier's Reach, of all places?"

He'd dreaded this moment. With the PLD-4000 staring him down, he would have no choice but to throw a friend under the bus. "I'd received information regarding the discovery of Iota particles in the Reach."

"The Iota particles. Who made you aware of them?"

"Commander David Ortega."

"The David Ortega stationed on Outpost Watchtower?"

"Yes." Jason hoped he hadn't put his friend in too much hot water.

Hariri checked over her data tablet. "Okay, now we've got that out of the way, let's start at the beginning. I'll need you to explain in your own words everything that happened from the moment the *Argo* received the distress call from the *UECS Vanguard*."

Jason bit into his piece of chocolate and prepared himself for what would be a very long discussion.

Outpost Watchtower

David knocked on the door, wondering what waited for him on the other side.

"Come," the voice instructed him.

He pushed it open slowly. At the far end of the luxurious quarters, Captain Lang stood by the viewport enjoying planet Delta-Hera IX's majestic panorama. He puffed away at a cigar while nursing a drink in a square-sided glass.

"Isn't cigar and scotch night Friday?" David approached him.

Lang passed him a filled glass and a fresh cigar.

David bit the end of his cigar off, and Lang lit it with his old lighter. The captain remained suspiciously quiet.

"What gives, sir?" David asked.

"I talked to Admiral Kostecki earlier." Lang puffed out a plume of smoke. "They've finished debriefing Jason Cassidy. He revealed—"

"That I'd given out the information regarding

the Iota particles before getting clearance." He took a sip of his drink. "I'm sorry. I should have asked you—"

"Admiral Kostecki has left it in my hands to discipline you accordingly."

David straightened his back.

"I fought in the war." Lang put his cigar down on the ashtray. "I know what it's like to lose colleagues. And friends." He stared into David's eyes. "Next time, ask me."

David breathed a sigh of relief. "Thank you, sir."

Lang frowned and picked up his cigar. "You're lucky you have such a soft captain."

To David he was far from soft. He was a fair and loyal man. "It won't happen again."

Lang gave him a knowing glance and a knock sounded at the door. "Come."

It opened, and Doctor Lenard stepped over the threshold, still in her surgical gear. Her eyes were bloodshot and her hair disheveled.

"Seems like you need one of these more than we do." Lang poured her a glass and handed it to her.

She promptly gulped it down.

"Will Tai live?" David asked.

"She will. I stopped the spread of damage from the wound on her leg." She passed the glass back to Lang for a refill. "But, she'll never walk again."

"Paraplegia?" Lang gave her another drink. "How's that possible? Isn't it a curable condition?"

"It is. But her body rejected all the regenerative

therapy I've thrown at it. She'll be able to live a productive life, but it will be from a wheelchair."

David shook his head in frustration. Lenard couldn't even tell them what had happened to Doctor Tai and why she was in her condition. The secrecy frustrated him no end.

"How's she taken the news?" Lang asked.

"She hasn't woken yet."

They shared a lengthy silence. The captain offered her another scotch, but Lenard waved it away.

She massaged her temples. "I'm going to have a shower and go to bed. I don't want to think about today anymore."

"Thank you for keeping us in the loop."

"Captain. Commander." She walked out and closed the door behind her.

Lang gazed at the smoke billowing from the end of his cigar. "I couldn't think of anything worse than being confined like that."

"Better than being dead..." David mused.

Lang didn't appear so sure, swishing the scotch around in his glass. He stopped and stared at him. He must've recognized the concern on his David's face. "What's on your mind, Commander?"

"Jason Cassidy." He frowned. "Doesn't all of this irritate you? Not knowing what the hell is going on over on the *Repulse*?"

Lang leaned back on the viewport. "I'd say it's better not to think about these things."

It wasn't really the advice David was after. "That's easier said than done. The man's a friend."

"I know." Lang filled up both their glasses. "Maybe a few more of these will help."

He wished the captain was right.

FIVE

UECS Repulse

Aly peered across the table at Commander Hariri and waited. All she wanted to do was get back to the ship and put everything that had happened behind her, but the *Repulse*'s XO seemed to be in no hurry.

"Alyssa Rycroft," Hariri finally said, putting down her data tablet. "Or do you prefer Aly?"

"Aly's fine."

"Good. Now, Aly, during this debriefing we'll be talking about everything that happened from the moment the *Argo* came to the aid of the *UECS Vanguard* through to the time you arrived here. Do you understand?"

Well, I'm not stupid.

"Yes."

"Excellent. On your ship's roster, you're listed as the engineer. Is that correct?"

"On our ship everyone has a few different jobs they—"

"But you primarily look after the ship's engines?"

"Yes."

Hariri documented it on her tablet. "I understand you worked with Professor Petit."

"After the first journey through the trans-space corridor, he assisted me with repairs. It was handy having an architect behind the Mark IV engine to help out."

"So, you and the professor discovered the Iota particles aboard the *Argo*?"

Aly chuckled. "It was Professor Petit who found them, but I was there."

Hariri perused her tablet again. "Would it be safe to assume while the professor was the brains behind getting the *Argo* home, you had some part in assisting him?"

"I guess, yeah."

"I would say that makes you an expert in the field, since you're the only two humans in existence to work with the new technology."

Aly narrowed her eyes. "I hadn't thought of it that way before. But I suppose I learned a lot from Professor Petit in the time I spent with him."

"Interesting."

Aly squirmed in her chair wondering why Hariri was so fascinated about the Iota particles and her relationship with the professor.

"In your experience, do you believe you could replicate a trans-space corridor?" the commander asked.

"Not a chance."

The light behind her flashed, and the warm glow of the PLD-4000 bathed the room in red.

Hariri raised her eyebrows. "Miss Rycroft, I need the truth."

A lump formed in Aly's throat at the commander's abruptness. While she hadn't thought she was lying, the PLD-4000 could detect someone being untruthful with themselves. She thought about the question again and her work with Petit.

"I guess if I stumbled upon similar conditions to the ones at Psi-Aion, I'd be able to use the same method employed by Professor Petit to reopen a trans-space corridor. However, for that to happen, someone else would need to construct the original corridor."

The red light blinked out, and Hariri appeared satisfied. "You got a firsthand look at the Seekers' weaponry when they attacked the *Argo*. As an engineer, what's your opinion?"

Aly had tried to put the memories of that day aside. "Isn't this something Professor Petit would be better off answering? I'm not sure I have the expertise in the area of—"

"Professor Petit covered the subject extensively in his debriefing, but it's always good to have another perspective from an accomplished engineer."

That's a nice way to butter me up.

"Their weapons are energy based," Aly said. "They can channel massive amounts of power and hit targets with pinpoint accuracy whether it be in open space or from orbit. As I recall the CDF have attempted to develop similar weapon in the past, but have failed."

"What about their defensive capabilities?"

"Not even a tritonium bombardment made a dent." Aly paused before continuing. "Ultimately, it was the weapon channeling the energy of the sphere that destroyed them."

"The sphere. How would you describe its power?"

Aly couldn't forget what it had done to an almost indestructible ship, making it collapse in on itself and disappear into nothing but vapors. "It's like reliving every nightmare you've ever had all at once."

Outpost Watchtower

Javier hated hospitals. As a man of science, it was a ridiculous fear. He'd concluded it was because whenever he was in one, it reminded him of his own mortality. And while he was only in his early sixties, and still considered a young man, he was closer to the end than not.

He approached a nurse walking out of a doorway. "Is she seeing any visitors?"

"You being here might be just what she needs," the flustered woman said to him. She motioned him toward the room, where inside lay Susan Tai.

"Susan," he whispered.

She didn't respond at first, keeping her eyes on the ceiling. But as he walked closer, her head turned ever so slightly.

"Javier?"

He took a seat at her bedside and put his hand on hers.

"I assume they've told you how the surgery went?" she said.

Javier nodded. He didn't know what to say. He didn't think telling her 'at least you're alive' would make her feel any better.

Her eyes darted to the other side of the room where an elaborate wheelchair sat. "They say it'll give me full mobility."

It seemed as much a relic of the past as the sphere discovered on Orion V. The fact that even biomechanical technology couldn't get her back on her feet spoke volumes of the weapons the Seekers wielded.

"While it's no consolation, Susan, your mind is—"

"What's the point of my mind when I can't walk around to use it?"

"One of the greatest intellects of the twentieth and twenty-first century was confined to a wheelchair for most of his adult life. He—"

"Yes, I know about Stephen Hawking," she sniped.

"And before regenerative therapy, other people in your condition led fulfilling and productive lives. If—"

"I don't think I'll be one of them, Javier." Susan sighed. "I don't have the strength."

"You'll have the full support of everyone at the Institute," Javier said, doing his best to smile. "You won't ever be alone."

A tear rolled down her cheek. "Ever since I was shot, I've been having dreams. Vivid dreams."

"That's only natural when something like this happens."

"I've been reliving things I never wanted to experience again." She wiped away her tears. "This morning when I woke, I was in a pool of my own sweat. I'd dreamed about what happened on Caeneus II."

"I don't believe you've ever told me about Caeneus II."

"I wouldn't have. It's not something I like talking about."

Javier sat quietly. He figured the best thing he could do for Susan now was to listen.

"It was in the first year of the war," she began. "I'd been on the *Vanguard* no more than three months. We got a call from an observation outpost on Caeneus II that they were being attacked by Centauri forces. I went down with a complement of Marines and got caught up in a firefight. We eventually took the outpost back but found no one alive."

Javier recalled hearing about it, but he had no idea Susan was there.

"We discovered the outpost's memory banks were stolen along with the fleet movements for five surrounding star systems. The call was made to follow the fleeing Centauri through the boggy swamps of the planet. Along the way, I fell down the edge of a cliff. I broke my leg and got stuck in the mud below. It was like quicksand. I couldn't move. I thought I was going to die." She stopped and looked straight into Javier's eyes. "I felt hopeless. I was in there for six hours. It wasn't until an engineering crew from the *Vanguard* came down to rig something to pull me out that I was free."

There was smile on her face before the sadness returned. "Nicolas was the one who pulled me out." She stared down at her crippled legs. "Once upon a time I would've said my work might get me through this, but I'm not sure that'll be the case anymore."

Javier knew Susan's career meant everything to her, so her speaking like that came as quite a shock. "What do you mean?"

"I mean, what's the point? Ever since Nicolas died..."

Javier frowned. She'd told him how her relationship with Captain Marquez had been rekindled on Psi-Aion. "Nicolas would've—"

"Come on, Javier, I was in the service, I get the whole speech about dying in the line of duty," she said bitterly. "If it wasn't for me, they never would've sent his ship to Orion V."

"And if I hadn't needed Kione," Javier said, "then you wouldn't have come. If a mining team didn't discover the sphere, then I wouldn't have left Earth. If Orion V wasn't feasible for mining, then the sphere would never have been discovered."

Susan glared at him.

"Life is full of variables that aren't in our control," he continued. "You can't get hooked up on—"

"Javier, I'm not in the mood for one of your lectures."

"I'm sorry." He'd been raised in a household of tough love and sometimes didn't know any better. "I do it because I care for you, Susan."

She burst out with more tears. "If that's the case, can I rely on you to help me?"

"Of course."

"Somewhere on Watchtower, or even the *Repulse,* you'll find a drug called cyclotrol."

"You can't be serious, Susan?" He stood from his chair, knowing full well what the drug was used for. "How could you ask that of me? You're not dying."

She tried to say something, but Javier cut her off. "What would you say if one of your patients asked this question?"

"Will you help me or not?" she bristled.

"No," he said adamantly. "I'll have no part in killing you."

"Then it's time for you to go, Javier." She turned her head away from him.

"Susan—"

"Leave!"

Javier walked out the door and slammed it shut behind him.

SIX

UECS Repulse

Conrad crossed his arms and stared at Commander Hariri while she tapped away at her data tablet. They'd split the *Argo* crew up and put them in separate quarters on their arrival, and his patience was wearing thin.

She finally placed the tablet down. "Mister Althaus, how long have you served aboard the *Cargo Ship Argo*?"

"Thirty-seven years."

"And how old were you when you began your tenure?"

He had to do the math in his head. "I was twenty-two."

Hariri picked up her tablet. "From what it says here, the *Argo* was purchased by Benjamin Cassidy, thirty-seven years ago, in secondhand condition."

"That's right."

"Benjamin Cassidy? The father of Jason and Tyler Cassidy?"

Conrad uncrossed his arms. "You obviously know the answers to these questions. Why—"

"Mister Althaus, please, I assure you there's a reason to every question I ask."

Conrad glared at the red light, realizing she was no doubt testing him so the validity of the mind-reading contraption would be accurate. He relented, wanting the experience to be over with. "Yes, he was their father."

"And your relationship with Benjamin Cassidy?"

"He was my brother. Half brother actually."

"And that's how you came into his employ?"

"We were partners."

The red light washed around the room. He glanced at it and frowned. While he'd always considered his brother a partner in the business, Benjamin Cassidy was the owner of the *Argo* and its cargo license. "I guess that thing knows everything. We weren't partners. He was the boss and I was his employee."

The red light vanished, and Hariri nodded. "Now, Mister Althaus, I'd like to ask you a few questions about your cargo business."

He raised an eyebrow. "Okay."

"I've been going through your logs. Under the code of the Commonwealth Shipping Network, it's a requirement to document all assignments with your licenser for tax purposes. Is that correct?"

"That's right," Conrad said, nervously.

"Now tell me, with all the jobs the *Argo* has had in

say the last five years, would you have logged them all with the CSN?"

"I don't see how this is relevant."

"Please, Mister Althaus, I need you to answer the question."

He kept his mouth closed, not wanting to play her games.

"In fact, it's common practice not to log certain activities with the CSN, isn't it? Most cargo ships do plenty of cash jobs." Hariri frowned. "Understand I'm not here to get you in trouble. I have no interest in your financials."

Then what are you interested in?

"Whatever you say won't be relayed to the CSN," she continued, "and once again, I remind you, you agreed to cooperate with us before this debriefing began."

Althaus rolled his eyes. "No, we haven't logged all our jobs with the CSN."

"Thank you." Hariri passed him her data tablet. "Can you confirm you were docked at Station Venicia for extensive hull repairs on this date."

He grabbed it and looked it over. "That sounds about right."

"It was in result of a pursuit in an asteroid field by this ship, was it not?" She leaned over and pressed a key to bring up the image of a Richmond Class freighter.

How does she know that?

"In fact, you and your crew had dealings with the

owners of this ship, *The Gallant Trader,* didn't you? Unlogged with the CSN because the owners in question were part of the infamous McKinley family. An arm of the Taurus crime syndicate."

Conrad stared at the vessel on the tablet, recollecting those days far too vividly and remembering the trouble the crew of the *Argo* had got into.

"Mister Althaus?" she pressed,

He slid the tablet back over to her. "Yes, we did."

"The dealings with them must have turned for the worst if this incident with them in the asteroid field is anything to go by. It seems you managed to fight another day, and luckily, a few months later the entire McKinley family were imprisoned with a long list of felonies. I don't suppose you know anything about that?"

Conrad knew all too well.

"Don't worry, you don't have to answer." Hariri smiled. "Okay, now let's talk about Orion V."

Outpost Watchtower

The crew lounge was a bevy of activity since Admiral Kostecki had given many of the *Repulse's* personnel permission for some R&R aboard the space station.

Javier stared through the viewport at Delta-Hera IX and the massive fleet carrier while it circled the outpost. It was the last place he wanted to be. But he needed a drink and didn't want to be alone in his quarters. Luckily, the raucous officers around him were stopping him from thinking too much. Though even with the noise, he couldn't get Susan out of his mind. What she'd asked of him was unconscionable. He'd never imagined she'd choose the easy way out. She'd had a magnificent career with CDF and the Institute. He didn't want to see her throw it away. He sipped on his scotch wondering if he'd consider something similar if he were in his situation.

A hand on his shoulder interrupted his train of thought and he glanced up at the man smiling over him. It took a moment for Javier to register the face. "Jonathan Avery?"

"Hello, Javier." His former colleague sat on the bar stool beside him. His hair had grayed, and there were wrinkles where there'd been none before, but it was still the same Jonathan Avery he remembered.

"How long has it been?" Javier asked him.

"I left TIAS after the Mark IV Project finished up. So—"

"That long?"

"That long..." Jonathan nodded. "What are you doing on Watchtower?"

"A complicated story you wouldn't believe, even if I could tell you."

"Ah, one of those. I remember them well."

Javier changed the subject. "Where did you end up? Last I heard you were hoping to get into the private sector."

"Money was always my weakness. I worked for a few good companies when I left, but I'm currently with

DestinyCorp. They design and manufacture satellites, probes, and drones, among other things."

Javier did indeed recall the man's love for cash. They'd spent many a wild night in Tokyo back in the day spending that money. "What are you working on at the moment?"

"The Destiny Resonance Telescope. That's why I'm here."

"Wasn't that supposed to be finished—"

"And installed years ago. Yes." Jonathan hailed down the barman and asked for a scotch of his own. "That was the main reason they built Outpost Watchtower, so we could point our gigantic telescope into Frontier's Reach and poke around it."

"But the war got in the way?"

"Right." Jonathan took his drink from the barman. "The commonwealth government partially funded the telescope and pulled their share when hostilities broke out. We sat in limbo until about eighteen months ago. They finally gave us the remaining funding, and here we are."

"So now you're installing it?"

"We've been here two weeks. Everything's hooked up, but we're having issues getting it connected to the station's power core." He took a sip of his drink and put it down, raising an eyebrow. "You wouldn't be interested in helping us look at it, would you?"

Javier stared out at the *Repulse* and wondered about Susan. "I've got a lot of things on my—"

"Come on, we could use the assistance. The guys

would get a real kick out of working with the famous Javier Petit."

Javier contemplated the invitation, wondering if it would take his mind of things. "Okay."

"Excellent." Jonathan slapped him on the shoulder. "It'll be just like the old days."

SEVEN

UECS Repulse

"You're the helmsman and doctor aboard the *Argo*?"

Kevin chortled at the astonishment in Commander Hariri's voice. "Helmsman, yes. Doctor, not so much. I heal bumps and bruises because I'm the most qualified."

"You're far too modest, Mister Rycroft. I see you served in the Colonial Medical Corps when you were younger," she read from her data tablet across the table from him.

"As a field medic only. I'm certainly no physician."

"Perhaps not, but regardless, the work you did during the incident with the Seekers is to be commended. I understand you assisted Doctor Tai in an autopsy."

"That's right. Our aim was to understand what control the Seekers had over the natives of Psi-Aion."

"We're you able to determine that?"

"No, we weren't." Kevin shook his head. "Doctor

Tai assumed they were using a technology completely foreign to us and undetectable to our scans."

"What's your opinion of their physiology?"

"It would be the opinion of an old medic only."

Hariri smiled. "As I've not yet debriefed Doctor Tai, your humble expertise will have to do."

"Well, all the data in the *Argo's* computers will tell you what you need to know. But basically, they're very much like us. Bipedal. Carbon based. They're skin and bone. Flesh and blood."

"In terms of development, where would you rate them compared to us?"

"At first, they appear to be hunter gatherers like early humans. However, as we discovered, the particular group we engaged with lived in a township. What's most interesting is their choice of weapons. Similarly to our descendants, they used spears but had also developed the bow and arrow, which on Earth was invented several thousands of years later."

"So, they're highly intelligent?"

"While I'm no anthropologist, they're definitely adaptable. For a length of time we weren't able to determine, the Seekers were coming down to their world and abducting their people. I guess in that time they came up with new methods to combat them."

Hariri nodded. "And why do you think they were so vital to the Seekers?"

Kevin had pondered the question a lot since the *Argo* returned home. "The Seekers were based at Psi-Aion for some time. They were using the moon as a base of operations to build their weapon. We never saw a real Seeker, so we can only assume they needed outside help to achieve their goals."

"Outside help?"

"Workers and soldiers. They even used Christian Nash as a liaison between them and us."

"What are your thoughts of the Seekers' true identity?"

"A mystery that may never be solved."

The rest of the debrief was exhausting. Kevin couldn't remember the last time he'd sat in one spot for so long. However, Commander Hariri was kind enough to bring him lunch halfway through. After hours of accounting every single moment he'd experienced on the *Argo*'s jaunt from Orion V to Psi-Aion and back, Hariri placed her data tablet in front of him.

"This document states everything that happened is to remain strictly confidential by order of the Ministry of Defense. I'm sure you understand if this information were to reach the public…"

Kevin believed in honesty and integrity. He didn't like the fact a government had the power to cover up something the public deserved to know, but realized he had little choice in the matter. He studied the fine print and placed his thumb on the data tablet, hopefully signing off on a chapter of his life he would never again have to relive.

"Thank you, Mister Rycroft." Hariri took back the tablet. "Before we wrap this up, I'd like to ask you a few questions about Jason Cassidy."

Kevin furrowed his brow. "Oh?"

"Nothing official, just an informal chat. He was once a member of the CDF who—"

"Had a decorated career during the war."

Hariri put her hands up in surrender. "No doubt, he'll always be remembered a hero, but with his dishonorable discharge he—"

"Wait. What?" Kevin's ears pricked up. "Dishonorable discharge?"

Hariri furrowed her brow. "You weren't you aware of this?"

His shoulders slumped, and he fell back in his chair. "No, I wasn't."

"You're back!"

Jason turned his head at the sound of Aly's voice as the door to the communal quarters opened, and Kevin walked in. Aly gave her father a hug who looked relieved to be reunited with everyone else after so long.

Althaus glanced up from the table, eating some cereal from a large bowl. "After our debriefs, they put us all together in here."

"Does that mean they'll let us go soon? Did Commander Hariri say anything?" Aly asked.

Kevin shook his head. "She said she'd tell us once they collate all our statements. They might have more questions."

"What else could they ask? The only question they

didn't was what brand of toilet paper we stocked on the *Argo*," Althaus quipped.

"I guess they'd be able to find that out while they're doing the repairs."

"And that's another thing. Why are we letting them have free rein on the *Argo*? Who knows what they're doing over there."

"The ship needs serious work," Jason said. "Us locking the door won't stop them erasing our computer banks of any evidence of our trip. We might as well take them up on their offer to fix the old girl."

"You might trust them; I don't."

"What makes you think I trust them?"

Althaus scoffed.

"What kind of questions did they ask you?" Aly asked Kevin, doing her best to break up the tension.

"Everything and anything."

"Standard procedure." Jason filled a glass of water from the drink dispenser and took a seat on the sofa in the living area of the quarters.

Kevin approached him. "You got a moment?"

Jason looked at him suspiciously, noticing Kevin made sure he was out of earshot of the others. "Sure."

"She asked about you."

"Who? Hariri?"

Kevin nodded and sat beside him.

"What did she want?" Jason asked.

"Nothing in particular. She mainly wanted to know how you handled yourself out there."

"What did you tell her?"

"That you should still be in the service."

"Well..." Jason chuckled, and the pair sat in silence for a few moments.

"Why didn't you tell me you were dishonorably discharged?"

Jason froze. Kevin's eyes bored straight into his. Since he'd arrived on the *Argo*, he'd told no one what had really happened after the war. "I guess you've caught me red-handed."

"Did you think any of us would care? We were always proud of you."

Jason looked away. "I suppose I thought you'd be ashamed of me."

"Come on, you know me better than that. Is it something you'd like to talk about?"

Jason scratched his chin, doing his best not to look at his first flight instructor in the eyes. "It's a story for another day."

"Well, okay. You always know where to find me for a chat." Kevin put a hand on his shoulder and left him be.

Jason stared into the abyss, once again reliving those final days before he'd been told he was no longer wanted.

EIGHT

UECS Repulse

Susan's eyes sprang open and her chest rose heavily. Sweat covered her from head to toe, and not for the first time made her feel as if she'd run through a tropical storm. With the darkness encompassing her, she couldn't remember where she was. That was until she pushed aside her sheets and her legs wouldn't move. She stared up at the ceiling and put her hands up as if it was collapsing in on her.

"Lights!"

The room illuminated and revealed the ward she'd been placed in when transferred from Outpost Watchtower. It was Doctor Lenard's hope that doing it sooner, rather than later, would help her transition easier for the long trip back to Earth.

The door creaked open.

"Are you okay, Doctor?" Nurse Freeman walked

toward Susan and picked up a fresh towel beside the bed to dab the sweat from her face.

Susan snatched it from her. "What time is it?"

"Oh-eight-twenty." Freeman frowned at the dampness of the towel. "Another nightmare?"

Susan knew Freeman wasn't deliberately condescending. But the last thing she wanted was to talk to a fleet nurse, half her age, about her bad dreams.

"We can schedule your bath earlier," Freeman offered.

Susan rolled her eyes. "I'm fine."

The nurse checked the readings on the medical monitor above the bed, seemingly content with what she saw. "I talked with Doctor Chang and Commander Hariri an hour ago. Admiral Kostecki has agreed to your visitor."

"What! Why didn't you tell me?"

"I'm sorry, Doctor, you were sleeping. You need all the rest you can get."

There's that condescension again.

"Look at me!" Susan snapped. "I've got plenty of time to rest."

"I can arrange the visit now, if you'd like?" Freeman said, keeping her cool.

Susan nodded.

It took another hour after the nurse left for him to arrive. When the door opened, she used her upper body strength to sit herself up. "Kione!"

He walked toward Susan, and the guard closed the door from the outside. "I'm sorry I took so long," he said.

"They had to shut down part of the ship so I could come here securely."

"Just imagine if the crew knew they had an alien on board."

"No doubt, once I return to Earth, everything will be as before, and I'll go back to the Institute with no one knowing of my existence."

Susan frowned. Kione had lived his whole life in confinement. The Institute was nice, and the habitat purpose-built for his needs was a phenomenal feat of engineering, but it was still a cage. She wished he was free but often wondered what would happen if humanity learned of his existence. Would they be ready for him? And if not, what would they do to him?

"Are they treating you well?" she asked.

"The admiral gave me my own quarters and cordoned off a section of the ship."

"Have they talked about putting you in cryo-stasis for the trip back to Earth?"

"Not yet."

"I imagine Doctor O'Malley will take over from me when you return. At least for the time being."

"I don't understand." He raised his eyebrows. "Why wouldn't you continue as head of staff?"

"Kione, I'll be in no condition to do my job anymore."

He looked over at the specialized wheelchair. "You've lost the use of your legs, but you'll be otherwise mobile with this device. Surely—"

"Stop, Kione. I had enough lecturing from Javier."

Susan stared into Kione's large eyes. She'd known him for four years and considered him family. "Sit down, please."

He did so, in the chair beside her bed.

"Do you remember me telling you about my time during the war on the *Vanguard*?"

He nodded. "Of course."

"Do you recall the story about the Siege of Maxima?"

"You found the crew of Maxima Station massacred, though some had survived."

"It was the most barbarous thing I'd ever seen." Susan closed her eyes. The images of the day were burned into her mind. "When I went in with the first relief team, those who were alive were hanging from the beams, pierced with steel hooks. It was like something from the dark ages. When we pulled them down, they were too far gone. I couldn't save them. There was one thing I never told you."

Susan reached out for Kione's hand, which he wrapped around hers. "During the war, CMOs in the field had permission to euthanize their patients if, in their medical estimation, they were beyond saving. However, there was a stipulation. The patient had to be of sound mind and had to request the treatment. It wasn't to be offered as an alternative." She frowned at the haunting reminder of the past. "Well, these poor officers all asked. I gave them a drug called cyclotrol. It was fast-acting and painless."

Kione eyed her suspiciously. "Why are you telling me this?"

"Because, Kione, I have a favor to ask." She cleared her throat. "I need you to find some cyclotrol for me."

Kione said nothing.

Damn him and his blank expressions.

"Say something," she pleaded.

He gripped her hand. "Humans raised me. Mentored me. I learned to understand how they valued life. What you ask of me is something—"

"Kione, I wouldn't request this of just anybody."

The pair sat in silence as the cogs turned inside Kione's mind. "Even if I did say yes, where would I get cyclotrol? From my understanding, the drug is now on the banned list."

"Trust me, every infirmary has it in stock. It's just a matter of finding it."

Kione sighed. "Doctor, this isn't a decision taken lightly."

"Take all the time you need."

But not too long.

Parliament House - Istanbul, Earth

"Mister President, can we get a comment on the latest polls?"

Glendon Jarret stepped from the presidential transport pod, onto the lawn, into a cavalcade of news reporters.

"Is there any chance your party might think about

replacing you before the next election?" another asked.

Glendon had fumed all morning since the *European Times* published their latest opinion polls. They'd been even worse than the ones in the *Martian Tribune*. His bodyguards pushed through the media men and women until Glendon found himself in the foyer of Parliament House.

"Couldn't they hold this off until tomorrow?" he said to his chief of staff who awaited him inside.

"*The Times* publish their polls the same day every month," Luan told him.

"Then maybe we should've scheduled my speech to the parliament yesterday."

"It wasn't sitting yesterday."

"I'm the president. They'll sit when I tell them to sit."

"While you can recall the ministers whenever you like, it would've looked odd to do so for something as arbitrary as these bills."

Luan was right. The media would've put two and two together and roasted him regardless. Glendon figured once he'd performed the inane duties he had at Parliament House, he'd sneak out of the back door. Though he shuddered to think how that would play in the evening news.

He walked down the corridor with Luan at his side, who promptly pulled out a data tablet. "Your speech is due to start at two p.m. Before that, there's a lunch with the Speaker and the party leaders at one."

"Fine. Fine."

"First we have a meeting scheduled with Minister Takashi in the Gladwyn Jebb Room."

Glendon turned left at the end of the corridor. "Good. I've wondered how things are progressing out there."

Luan pushed the door in for him, and there waiting in the room at the large table was the Minister of Defense.

"Mister President." Takashi put his data tablet down and stood.

"Mister Takashi." Glendon took a seat opposite him. "What have you got to report?"

"Quite a lot actually." Takashi slid the data tablet across to him.

Glendon read over it while Takashi told him everything that had come out of the debriefs with Professor Petit and the crew of the *Argo*.

Glendon couldn't help but be shocked. Seekers. Aliens on a planet three hundred light-years away. Kione's mental abilities. A new form of FTL travel. A weapon of incalculable power.

"Well, this is something, isn't it?" He turned to Luan. "Thoughts?"

"Historic would be the word that comes to mind," his chief of staff concluded.

"True, however, with Kione, we've known about the existence of extraterrestrials for some time."

"But this is very different."

Glendon couldn't argue. "To cover up the discovery and continuing study of Kione is one thing. To keep this genie in the bottle will be quite another. We also still have what happened at Orion V to deal with."

"What are your instructions, Mister President?" Takashi asked.

Glendon put the data tablet down on the table. "Well, we can all agree this has to stay under wraps. If the public ever got wind of it..." He trailed off, knowing he didn't need to continue. "I want Professor Petit back here as soon as possible. He'll have a lot of work on his plate when he returns."

"The *Repulse's* journey to Earth will take six months," Takashi said.

"I also want Kione on that ship. With everything that's happened, his study is now of paramount importance."

"And Doctor Tai?"

"Hmm? Oh, the crippled doctor. Yes, her, too."

Takashi tapped his hand on the desk. "And what about the crew of the *Argo*?"

"Have they signed nondisclosure agreements?" Luan asked.

"Of course."

"All of which are useless. These are civilians. Too many people already know about this." Glendon stared at Luan who glared back at him in equal measure.

Glendon turned to Takashi. "I assume you've mobilized the Zero-Five operatives?"

The Minister of Defense nodded.

"Tell them they have new orders. The crew of the *Argo* are to be eliminated."

NINE

Outpost Watchtower

Javier had never seen a telescope of Destiny's complexity or technological design. It wasn't as physically large as others he'd observed, but if what Jonathan Avery had said was true, its range alone would surpass anything ever imagined.

"Javier!"

He turned from the viewport where the cylindrical-shaped module protruded from the hull of the space station, to find Jonathan approaching him.

"What do you think of my baby?" he asked Javier.

"It looks impressive. The question is, can it be made to work?"

"It'd want to. I've staked my reputation on it. Not to mention a lot of DestinyCorp's money."

"Well, let's see if we can't keep your name in check."

"Come." Jonathan directed him over to the inner

workings of the telescope. "This is what we call the underbelly."

The great expanse reminded Javier of the engine room of a small ship. Large pylons connected the resonance telescope with the outpost's outer hull, while power conduits weaved between the telescope and the power systems of the station. Around the various maintenance junctions were Jonathan's staff, who busily went about their work.

"You were saying you were having trouble channeling the power from the station to the telescope?"

Jonathan nodded. "Our first trial sent a surge through the telescope that nearly blew the thing to kingdom come."

Heads popped up from the junctions and followed the pair walking through the section.

"Well, we don't want a repeat of that, do we?" Javier stopped and touched one of the insulated conduits. "At least you're using the best equipment."

"Have you ever known me to skimp?"

Javier chuckled, and they continued toward a maintenance junction where a team of three were working on the telescope's computer components.

"Professor Petit," Jonathan said. "I'd like to introduce you to Mister Caruso."

The young team leader stopped what he was doing, and his eyes lit up. "Professor Petit! It's such an honor." He put out his hand and shook Javier's. So much so, Javier thought the excited technician would shake it off. The others followed with equal jubilance.

"Professor Petit's here to help us with our problem."

The trio looked at each other with wide smiles. While under normal circumstances most people would be insulted at someone coming in at the eleventh hour, these awestruck youngsters didn't seem to care in the least. In the past, Javier enjoyed having his ego stroked, but with all that had happened of late, there were now more important concerns in life.

"Well, I'll leave you to it," Jonathan said. "Lunch at twelve-thirty in the crew lounge?"

Javier nodded, and Jonathan left him and the team to search for a fix to their issue. "So, tell me, where are the power overloads occurring?"

Caruso led him over to the main conduits and eyed him like he was a big-time sports star. Javier tried not to be rude, but the thought of spending the next few days with starstruck technicians straight out of college didn't appeal to him.

He thought about Alyssa Rycroft. She needed no degree. She had to be good at what she did, otherwise her ship didn't fly.

What I wouldn't give to have her here right now.

UECS Repulse

Jason had never met Admiral Kostecki, but his first impression peering into the cold blue eyes of the man, told him he wasn't someone to be messed with.

"Mister Cassidy for you, Admiral," Hariri said, escorting Jason into the *Repulse's main office*.

"Yes, thank you." Kostecki nodded. "That'll be all."

The commander turned and exited, closing the door behind her.

Kostecki put his hands together on his desk. "I was talking to Captain Kaufman a few days ago? We've been friends for as long as I can remember."

Jason furrowed his brow. "I hardly believe I've been called here to discuss my past transgressions, Admiral. At least I hope not."

Kostecki continued to study him like he was an insect to be squashed, but Jason stood his ground, not letting the Admiral intimidate him. "No, I guess I didn't. Sit down, Mister Cassidy."

Jason sat on the chair opposite the desk.

"Command and the Ministry of Defense finished checking over your statements this morning." Kostecki read from his data tablet. "They're satisfied with everything you've told us."

"It would've been difficult to lie with a PLD-4000 pointed at our heads."

"You would realize more than most their use is standard practice in situations such as these."

Was that a dig?

"Well, I suppose you're right."

"Now, you've all signed binding nondisclosure agreements. I assume I don't need to remind you of the importance of upholding them."

"Not at all."

"Or the penalties for breaking the agreement. While you may have got away with your last misdemeanor in the service, if you step out of line this time..." Kostecki paused before continuing. "Suffice to say, treason isn't looked upon favorably with the current administration."

"Got it."

The admiral glanced back at his data tablet. "With that understood, your ship has been repaired, and you and the rest of your crew are free to leave."

"That's very generous of you, Admiral." It sounded more sarcastic than Jason would've liked, considering he was doing his best not to antagonize Kostecki. All Jason wanted to do was get off the damn carrier. "Thank you for your hospitality."

Cargo Ship Argo

Jason stepped into the engine room to find Aly and Kevin standing over the maintenance console.

"All right, how did our friends go repairing the old girl?" he asked them.

"It's amazing. They've replaced all the parts that needed fixing with newer designs. Look at this." Aly pointed at the console. "These energy converters were giving me trouble for years. I had to rebuild them because of how rare and expensive they are. They're now the top-of-the-line models. They should last at least five years if serviced regularly."

"Well, I'm glad someone's happy." He walked closer to them. "Make certain you go over all the changes they made. If there's something here that shouldn't be, let me know."

"What am I searching for exactly?" she asked.

"I'm not sure. But you know this ship back to front. If there's something out of place, you'll find it."

"Okay."

Jason exited the engine room and Kevin followed him out. "How soon can we be out of here?"

"Give me an hour to do the preflight checks, and we'll be on our way," Kevin told him. "Has Outpost Watchtower given us clearance for docking?"

"We're not going to Watchtower."

"I assumed you'd want to see your old friend from the *Raptor*." They walked on to the bridge where Althaus was checking over the workstations.

"I talked to him over a commlink when they let us out. But since we're unable to discuss what happened with Nash and anything else, I didn't see much point cutting into our travel time."

"What course do you want me to plot?"

"Vesta III. I'm going home."

Kevin's face went pale.

"I'm sure you'll be able to find some business along the way," Jason said to Althaus, who appeared to do everything to hide his glee.

TEN

UECS Repulse

Scans, scans, and more scans.

Since coming aboard from the *Argo* and being taken into custody, Kione had been poked, prodded, and probed by every medical instrument imaginable. The *Repulse's* Chief Medical Officer had instructions to give TIAS updated studies, with all that had happened since being with the Seekers. Unfortunately, Doctor Chang had no expertise with his biology. She'd never worked on a member of his species before, let alone any other form of extraterrestrial life.

She seemed fascinated by him, but her bedside manner was cold and uncaring. Kione felt like something from a petri dish instead of an intelligent living being.

Being strapped down in an enclosed tubular biochamber in darkness was something he hadn't missed since leaving the Institute. His thoughts drifted to Tai and what she'd asked of him. He wondered what she would have said if he'd been the one to come to her with the same request. He couldn't imagine her saying yes.

So why am I considering it?

Is it because I'm not human?

He didn't know whether it made a difference. He questioned if there was something in his DNA that made him think ending one's existence early was acceptable.

Or has the sphere done something to me?

Kione had already struggled to comprehend the powers he'd developed when in the vicinity of the ancient device. And why those abilities were now gone.

Maybe it's just another question I'll never have an answer to.

The bio-chamber lit up around him, bathing him in light. The conveyance slid outward, and in moments he was back out in the infirmary with Doctor Chang standing over him, yanking off his restraints.

"You can get up," she told him.

Kione pulled himself upright and swung his legs off the chamber bed. He looked at the monitor above to check over the scans, while Chang filed them into a data tablet, preparing them for someone a little more qualified to review.

She pointed to the bed in the center of the infirmary. "Sit down, please."

Kione walked over to it, and a voice rang out over the speakers.

"Doctor Whistler to Doctor Chang."

She activated the intercom on the bulkhead panel. "Doctor Chang here."

"Those lab results have come in."

"Already?"

"The clock's ticking. We'll have ten minutes to review them before the sample disperses."

"Okay, I'll be right there." Chang placed down her data tablet and a small medical probe on the bed next to Kione. She marched out into the corridor, telling the guard outside the door to lock it behind her, without so much as saying goodbye.

Kione stared around the sterile infirmary and stopped when a closed cabinet caught his eye. On it was a label in bold text: PHARMACEUTICALS.

He stood from the bed and sauntered over to it, glancing at the door to make sure the coast was clear. He opened the cabinet where inside were rows upon rows of medicines, all in small containers and tubes. He worked his way from the top shelf downward, until he reached the drugs beginning with C. There were only a few vials of it, but the label was clear as day: Cyclotrol.

While he hadn't decided yet whether he'd grant Tai's request, if he did, it'd be unlikely another opportunity would arise to procure it.

The door to the infirmary clicked, unlocking from the outside and Kione grabbed the vial, stashing it inside his pants pocket. With a flick, he closed the cabinet, and Doctor Chang walked in.

Kione put both his hands in his pockets and stared at the ceiling as casually as he could.

Chang eyed him suspiciously and then gestured toward the bed. "Let's continue."

Holden City, Mars

Marissa Caldwell finished her bowl of cereal and placed it in the dish recycler. Through the kitchen window, the stars of the dark, early morning sky shone through Holden City's domed enclosure. She loved her work but hated the hour she had to be out of bed. Someone had to write the news though, and it was the only thing she ever grew up wanting to do.

"What are you still doing here?"

She turned to find Marcus staring at her, wearing only a pair of shorts. She never got sick of looking at his chiseled physique in the morning. Or any other time of the day for that matter.

"My alarm went off late. I'll be there with plenty of time." Her boss wouldn't care. With the amount of extra hours she worked, she hadn't earned the nickname Super Woman for nothing.

Marissa grabbed Marcus by the buttocks and pulled him in close. They kissed, and she glanced toward the bedroom.

No, I can't be that late.

She sighed and picked up her bag.

"When do you think you'll be home?" he asked.

"Five at the latest."

"So, six then?"

"I'll do my best."

They kissed once more, then she slung her bag over her shoulder and walked out of the apartment.

She hurried at a brisk pace to the Beenleigh Street Station, not wanting to miss the four fifty-three service into the city center. The train stopped on the platform just as she jogged up the steps. She flung her bag through the doors, stopping them from closing. And pulled them open, throwing herself inside.

With the near-empty carriage practically all to herself, she had her choice of almost any seat she wanted. Of the two people with her, one was asleep stretched out over a row of three seats, while another sat across from her patting what was once a frozen chicken meal with a leash tied around it.

Marcus hated her traveling to work on the train. Marissa's excuse was that she wanted to gauge the people of the large Martian city. Unfortunately, in the initial hours of the morning, the only thing she could glean was Holden City still had serious homeless and mental illness problems.

She stepped off the train at the City Center Station and walked down to her work building. It was one of the tallest on Mars, except for a few glitzy apartment towers, which housed the wealthy.

"Marissa, it's not like you to be this late," Janine, the early morning receptionist said as she entered the office. "Did that man hunk of yours want to keep you all to himself?"

Marissa loved Janine. She always made her laugh.

"Yes, but that's not the reason I'm late. Have there been any calls for me?"

"Not yet."

"Okay." Marissa knew there'd be plenty of messages waiting for her when she logged on to her computer.

She walked past the reception area and into the giant bullpen that housed the news reporters of the *Martian Tribune*—the most read paper on Mars, and one of the most influential in the entire commonwealth. Through the banks of empty cubicles, she approached her work domain and threw her bag down on her desk. Her computer autoloaded with her presence and she quickly discovered she'd been right. There were seventy-three messages waiting for her. Marissa scrolled down the list. Most were appointments with interviewees she'd organized days earlier. Some were messages from her sources. And others were tips from random individuals.

Her eyes stopped at the bottom of the list and she did a double take. It wasn't a name she'd seen in a very long time. She read through the message and opened the hefty data file that came along with it.

What the hell?

She pressed the intercom on her desk. "Janine, how long until Sandra's in?"

"She's not due for another hour."

"Let me know the moment she walks in the building."

"Sure thing."

She's not going to believe this.

ELEVEN

Cargo Ship Argo

"Cargo Ship Argo *you're clear to depart.*"

The communications officer of the *Repulse* gave Jason the permission they'd needed. "Get us the hell out of here," he said.

Kevin nodded. "Course plotted for Vesta III."

The *Repulse*, Outpost Watchtower, and Delta-Hera IX rapidly disappeared into the distance.

Jason tapped the intercom on the console beside his chair. "Buckle up, everyone. Prepare for FTL." He allowed a few moments for Althaus and Aly to get settled in below deck and directed Kevin to hit the gas. With a push of the large lever on the helm, the *Argo* erupted beyond the speed of light.

Once the hull vibrations returned to normal. Jason unclasped his harness and left the bridge in Kevin's capable hands. He walked to the stern, toward the engine room, where Aly was hard at work in the maintenance junction.

"How did you go with your search?" he asked her.

"I'll let you know if I find anything," she said without looking up.

"Thanks." He moved to the exit before spinning back around.

Something's not right.

Jason put his hand on the hatchway. "What's up with you?"

"Nothing."

"Seriously?"

"I'm fine."

He stepped toward her. "Aly?"

She slammed a spanner down beside her, and jumped out of the junction with a deadly fire filling her eyes. She shut the lid firmly on her toolbox and its sound echoed around the engine room. "Remember when we were heading to Frontiers Reach, and I asked you to stay on the ship once this was all over?"

Jason vaguely remembered the conversation.

"You may not have said it, but you made me believe you'd think about it actually remaining on board," she continued. "I knew you were lying, of course, but with everything that happened at Psi-Aion, I thought maybe there'd be a chance you might reconsider."

Jason tried to open his mouth to say something, but Aly cut him off. "Don't you feel some responsibility?"

He attempted to speak again.

"Well?" she pressed.

"Are you going to let me talk or not?"

Aly relented and crossed her arms. "Go ahead."

"Wouldn't you rather this ship was run by someone who wants to be here?"

"What's stopping you from wanting to be here?"

Jason leaned back on the maintenance console. "Aly, my family's gone. My mom, my dad, and now my brother. You guys were going along fine until I came back. Look at the havoc I've left in my wake."

"But we're your family too. Perhaps not by blood—"

"And what'll happen to you if I stay?"

Aly rolled her eyes. "What do you think, you're some voodoo curse or something?"

"Well, it's as good an explanation as anything I've heard so far."

"Such a moron." Her voice softened, and she stepped closer to him. "I think you're just afraid."

It was Jason's turn to roll his eyes. "Afraid of what?"

Aly didn't have an immediate answer. Instead, she wrapped her hands around his neck and kissed him. Jason wasn't sure how to react. He let his lips decide for him and kissed her back

Whoa...

They parted and stared at each other. He didn't know what to say. And either did she by the look of it.

Out of the corner of Jason's eyes, a figure emerged. He and Aly looked at Althaus standing before them with his mouth agape.

"I remembered there was something I had to do down in the cargo bay." Aly blushed and, as quick as a flash, hurried off from the awkward situation, brushing past Althaus through the hatchway.

"What is it, Althaus?" Jason asked him, regaining his composure.

His older comrade eyed Aly running toward the elevator then turned back around. "Rycroft said I'd find you here. We need to talk about the ownership of this ship."

Jason had a decision to make. Would he give it to Althaus who probably deserved it as he was the closest thing to family he had left? Or hand it over to Kevin because Althaus was such a bastard? It wasn't a choice he was in the mood to make right at that moment. "Let's take a rain check and come back to that."

He walked from the engine room, wondering what in the world had just happened before his uncle walked in.

Holden City, Mars

Marissa sat in her cubicle, staring at her computer monitor. She was trying to write an article she'd planned for tomorrow's paper. It was a puff piece that she couldn't get enthused about.

It'd been over half a day since she'd handed over the information about her tip-off and wondered how long Sandra needed to make her mind up. Having waited long enough, she hurried through the bullpen to her editor's office, and knocked on her door.

"Come in."

Marissa pushed it open to find behind her desk, sifting through some files on her computer, the editor in chief of the *Martian Tribune*, Sandra Veroni. Marissa's boss didn't even blink. She continued to stare at her monitor for several more seconds before looking up and adjusting her eyes.

"Close the door," she finally said.

Marissa did so and took a seat opposite her. "Well?"

"Well..." Sandra mused. "It's an interesting piece of writing."

"It's an interesting piece of writing?" Marissa chuckled. "That's all you've got to say?"

"What do you want me to say?"

"How about: Hey, can you get cracking on that story so it's ready for the front page of the *Tribune*'s evening edition?"

"How can I run with this?" Sandra stood and walked over to the window. "You can't substantiate it, and if it's fake, we'll be in serious breach of the media standards charter. If it's true, we'll royally piss off the current standing administration."

"Since when do we care about that?" Marissa got up from her seat and approached her. "We're here to report the truth. We've got a story about a cover-up thirty years in the making. Not to mention information on a massacre this government has yet to reveal to the public. We have to make them accountable."

"And end up like the *Continental Herald*?"

Marissa threw her arms up in the air and walked away. Like everyone else, she'd heard of the sackings after the Earth-based newspaper ran a story on the final assault of Centauri by Earth forces at the end of the war. One that hadn't painted President Jarret in the greatest of lights. Many rival newspapers assumed the *Herald* was leaned on by his administration to clean up their house because of it, or face increased scrutiny on their coverage.

"All the more reason to run the story," Marissa continued. "If this administration is rotten, let's get to the bottom of it."

"I can't risk the *Tribune's* reputation." Sandra shook her head. "I'm sorry, Marissa."

She stared at Sandra, not knowing whether to be angry or bemused.

So, this is what journalism has come to?

Marissa stormed out of the office and went to her cubicle, where she shut down her computer, and picked up her bag.

The first sight she saw when she entered her apartment after returning home was Marcus preparing a roast in the kitchen.

He looked at his wristwatch in mock horror. "And what time do you call this? I didn't expect you back for hours."

"Bad day." She dropped her bag on the counter and sat on the stool opposite him.

Marcus promptly opened the wine refrigerator and grabbed a bottle of chardonnay. He poured her a glass and handed it to her.

She smiled. At least she tried to. "What would I do without you?"

He leaned over the counter and kissed her on the forehead. "Go and rest. I'll let you know when dinner's ready."

Marissa kissed him back and took her wine through to the living area where she sat on the sofa and drank slightly larger gulps than she should have. The day's frustration burned inside her. Not just that Sandra had robbed her of the story of the century but how her industry had sunk so low.

I could take things into my own hands.

It might be the greatest thing I ever do.

Or it may get me fired...

She finished off her glass of wine and tapped her fingers on the arm of the chair.

Oh, what the hell.

She activated the wall monitor and stared down the lens of the camera. "Hello, my name is Marissa Caldwell..."

TWELVE

Cargo Ship Argo

Jason took the hot meal out of the food dispenser and breathed in the peppercorn sauce wafting through the air. It may not have been the real thing, but it was the best he'd get out on the frontier.

He sat at the table, picked up a knife and fork, and remembered back to his days in the service. Even during the war he'd eaten better than he had his whole life aboard the *Argo*. But there was just something about the rehydrated meals he'd grown up with that made him nostalgic.

A shadow appeared over him and he turned to find Althaus standing at the door of the galley.

"What?" Jason said to him, not too impressed with being interrupted.

Kevin emerged from behind Althaus and frowned. "Sorry, Jason. Althaus was insistent we get to the matter of the *Argo's* ownership."

"Does it have to be right now? We've got six months until I hop off at Vesta III."

"If we don't do it, it'll never get done." Althaus walked toward him and leaned over, putting his hands on the chair opposite. "I know you, kid. You'll drag this out."

Any chance you can stop calling me kid? That might help your cause.

"It's something that'll take time to think about," Jason said.

"What's there to think about? If you hadn't come along, I was the next in line. It's only fair—"

"But Tyler didn't leave it to you, did he?" Jason threw his fork down. "Why do you deserve it?"

Althaus stood upright and fumed. "Because I'm your father's half brother."

"So, because Grandpa banged a different grandma, you think that gives you a claim to the *Argo*?"

Atlhaus's face reddened and Jason looked to Kevin who was doing his best to stay out of the argument.

"What about you?" he asked him, with a tone he didn't mean to be so adversarial. "What's your pitch?"

"I have no pitch, Jason." Kevin ambled over to the drink dispenser and got himself a glass of water. "Tyler left the ship to you. It's your decision."

Jason was well aware Kevin didn't want the *Argo*, but in his heart he probably didn't want to work for Althaus either.

"Maybe I should do what Solomon did." Jason

sliced the steak with his knife. "I'll cut the ship in two and give you a piece each."

"You're an idiot," Althaus grumbled.

"Leave it with me, okay. I promise I'll have a decision by the end of the week."

Althaus went to say something but was interrupted by Aly's call over the intercom.

"Bridge to Jason."

Jason activated his commband. "Go ahead."

"A bogey's appeared at the edge of scanning range. It's altered course and heading our way."

Jason narrowed his eyes and the trio headed to the bridge, to find Aly sitting at the operations station.

The bogey was indeed pursuing the *Argo*, and it was catching them fast.

"How long before they reach us?" Jason asked her.

"Three hours at this rate."

Kevin eyed the monitor. "Any transponder ID?"

Aly shook her head. "It's running dark."

"Marauders?" Althaus pondered.

"We're not that far away from Outpost Watchtower. It'd take some serious gonads to hit even a civilian ship so close to a fleet carrier. Marauders aren't stupid." Jason leaned over and activated a star chart of the region on an opposing monitor. He pointed at one of the stars. "The Verada System. If it is Marauders, we'll need cover. We'll be a sitting duck out in open space."

Kevin nodded. "It'll take a slight detour, but we can be there before they reach us."

"Alter course."

Kevin trotted off to the helm and to make the necessary correction while Althaus made his way to the systems station.

Jason and Aly caught a glimpse of each other. They hadn't really spoken since their episode in the engine room, and she'd avoided him like the plague. While he wanted to say something, the time wasn't right. They now had more pressing matters to attend to.

Holden City, Mars

Sandra didn't even consider putting on something nice for the evening. Her day had been long. Too long. It was straight into her pajamas. She stepped out of the bathroom with a towel wrapped around her head and entered the kitchen to rummage in the pantry.

"Ty, did you eat the last of the chocolate?" she shouted toward the living area.

He didn't reply.

"Ty!"

She stormed out of the kitchen to find her husband on the sofa with his eyes glued to the wall monitor. "Did you hear me?" she asked.

"Have you seen this?" He pointed at the news report. A 'breaking news' banner scrolled across the bottom of the screen.

"This video by Marissa Caldwell of the Martian Tribune *just posted to the ComChat network has already gone viral,"* the anchor said.

Sandra sat on the arm of the sofa, while a video played of Marissa sitting in her own apartment.

"Hello, my name is Marissa Caldwell—journalist at the Martian Tribune *in Holden City. I come to you today with a report my employers fear releasing. Our profession has always strived to work for the people and give you the news, warts and all. But now, with the current administration, we've become frightened. Frightened for our careers and our livelihoods. This must change. They will cast a shadow on us no longer.*

"This morning I received information that an aggressor of extraterrestrial origin attacked the decium ore mining facility on Orion V. All lives were lost, including the crew of the UECS Vanguard, *which was delivering another extraterrestrial to the planet to be used in the study of an ancient artifact unearthed beneath the surface over a year and a half ago.*

"When was President Jarret going to inform the families of those lost? When was he going to reveal the existence of an extraterrestrial covered up for over thirty years? Or tell us of the six million-year-old relic beneath Orion V?"

Sandra's commband lit up with messages coming in from the powers that be at the *Tribune*. "I'm going to kill her."

"It's time we heard from President Jarret. The ball's in your court, Mister President. What do you say to the people of the commonwealth?"

THIRTEEN

Cargo Ship Argo

Aly checked the scanners on the operations console at the Verada system. It consisted of four large-mass objects. Two minor planets near the sun and two big gas giants toward the outer edge of the system.

Jason walked up from behind her. "Verada IV seems nice."

The fourth planet was a gas giant only slightly smaller than Jupiter. Its atmosphere contained elements of hydrogen, helium, methane, and ammonia.

"We probably wouldn't want to go on vacation there," she quipped.

"It'll just be a stopover." Jason turned to Kevin. "Take us to Verada IV."

He nodded and altered the *Argo's* heading toward the large blue orb. All the while, Aly kept an eye on the outer edge of the system, waiting for their pursuer to appear.

"Approaching the fourth planet," Kevin said.

"Initiate orbital insertion." Jason stroked his shabby beard. "Hightail it to the opposite side of the planet. Let's see if they enjoy playing hide and seek."

Aly wasn't so sure his plan would succeed. The math didn't work. She imagined Jason knew that, too, and hoped he had another idea.

Kevin began his countdown. "We'll be out of their scanning range in seven...six...five...four—"

An alert rang out from Aly's console. "Damn it! They dropped out of FTL just before we took cover. It's a fair chance they would've calculated our heading."

"Did you get a good scan?" Jason sat down in the captain's chair. "What are we dealing with?"

She brought up the familiar Richmond Class freighter on her monitor, and her heart skipped a beat. "Oh no."

"Oh no?"

"It's *The Gallant Trader*," Althaus said, checking the scans from his station.

"Who's the gallant trader?" Jason asked.

"*The Gallant Trader* is a ship not a person."

"Right. And who—?"

Kevin spun around. "It's the flagship of the McKinley family."

"The McKinleys? The crime mob?"

Aly nodded. "We worked for them in the past. It's a long story. Last we heard of them, they were all in prison."

"They may have someone on the outside working for them," Althaus added.

Jason glared at him. "What do you mean?"

"I don't know. It's just... Hariri asked me about our dealings with the McKinleys during my debrief. It seems a coincidence that suddenly they should reappear."

Jason appeared to believe so, too. "Well, regardless, they're here. We need to get creative." He turned to Aly. "How do you think we'll go inside that?" He gestured toward Verada IV.

"Inside the atmosphere?" She looked again at the composition of the giant world's nasty environment. "It wouldn't be my first idea—"

"Have you got a better one?"

She studied her monitor and ran the computations. "Don't go any farther than two kilometers down."

"You heard her, Kevin, take us down."

He glanced at Jason warily and dipped the *Argo* toward the planet. Its hull rattled and screeched. Aly could almost feel the pain of the old girl as she wailed out in agony. Her father leveled the ship off and nuzzled it between a pair of volatile gas layers.

Then the wait began.

Apart from the occasional rumble, the *Argo* didn't budge.

That was until a torpedo exploded off her port bow.

Boom!

Everyone launched from their seats and sparks flew from the ceiling. The lights flickered and Aly looked upward from the deck, wondering how she'd got there. She quickly regained her senses and pulled herself up.

"How the hell did they pinpoint us so quickly?" Althaus bellowed from the other side of the bridge, while another torpedo detonated off the starboard bow.

Jason grappled at his chair, heaving himself back in to it. "Kevin, alter course. Any direction! Aly, are you sure you looked everywhere when we left the *Repulse*?"

"What does that have to do with..." Aly raised her eyebrows, the realization dawning on her. "A homing beacon?"

Another torpedo shook the ship off its axis and the ship spun around like an old washing machine.

"We can't keep doing this!" Kevin yelled out, stabilizing the helm.

"Where would you place a homing beacon so no one could find it?" Jason asked her.

Aly pondered the question, and a thought popped into her head. "I'll be in the engine room!"

Caput Mundi House - Istanbul, Earth

"It's time we heard from President Jarret. The ball's in your court, Mister President. What do you say to the people of the commonwealth?"

"Turn it off!" Glendon pounded his fist onto his desk, while Luan Ntini deactivated the large wall monitor at the end of the office. "How the hell did this get out?" he stared across at his chief of staff and then shot an accusatory glare at his Minister of Defense.

"We kept a close eye on all communications from the *Repulse* and Outpost Watchtower," the dumfounded Takashi said. "There has been no leak of information."

"Well, it got out somehow. You've been asleep at the wheel, Takashi." Glendon scowled at Luan. "This won't play out well at all. If I wasn't already toast at next year's election, I will be now. How are we going to fix this?"

Luan frowned. "Since Caldwell did this on her own accord, we can't go after the *Tribune* like we did with the *Herald*."

"And we can't make her disappear, it'll look too suspicious."

"We could try to defame her," Takashi suggested. "The information she has might be disseminated and made to appear fake. And if—"

"I'd advise against that," Luan interrupted him. "If we're found out, losing an election will be the least of our worries."

Damn Luan and his logic.

Glendon had found himself caught between a rock and a hard place, but during his career he'd always turned the tables and used it to his advantage. "Get Ryland in here. We need to get on the front foot and put a presser out immediately."

"How do you intend to play this?"

"One step at a time." Glendon glanced at Takashi. "Have our team of Zero-Five operatives completed their mission?"

"Last they informed me they were about to engage the *Argo* in the Verada System."

"Get onto your people. They have new orders."

Cargo Ship Argo

"We need to go lower!" Another torpedo detonated near the hull, rocking Jason around in his seat.

"If we do—"

"Do it!" Jason ordered Kevin, cutting him off. "Take us a click farther down."

The helmsman relented and dropped the *Argo* lower still.

Jason tapped the intercom to the engine room. "Have you found that homing device yet?"

"Stand by!" Aly replied

"We can't—"

An additional discharge pushed the ship to port. "One more and we're done," Althaus said from the systems station.

"Aly!"

The shaking suddenly subsided and silence permeated around the bridge. Jason darted his eyes about waiting for the next blast.

But it never came.

"Well done, Aly." Jason let himself slide into the back of his chair. "Good work."

"I didn't do anything."

"What?"

"I've found the homing device. They attached it in-

side the FTL core. Ingenious really. No wonder I didn't find it. But it'll take a while to remove."

"Then why have they stopped firing?"

"They may think we've been destroyed."

"Possibly."

"Hull pressure's at maximum," she said, urgently. *"We have to get out of this soup now!"*

"Very well." Jason nodded to Kevin. "Take us up."

The *Argo* rose through the gaseous clouds of Verada IV, and the blue haze around them turned into the dark backdrop of stars. But the pursuing ship was nowhere to be seen.

"Where are they?" Jason asked.

"I'm picking up a bogey." Althaus read off the scanners. "To port."

The *Argo* circled with Kevin's deft touch to find the Richmond Class freighter eyeballing them.

Jason shook his head. "The bastards just waited us out."

"Why aren't they firing?" Kevin wondered.

"I don't know. Maybe they're pausing for dramatic effect."

The Gallant Trader moved to starboard and maneuvered away, leaving everyone on the bridge to stare blankly through the viewport.

"What just happened?" Althaus asked.

"Right now it doesn't matter." Jason activated the intercom. "Aly, how are you going with that beacon?"

"Still trying to take it out."

"Scrap that. Just get the FTL up and running. I assume we need to make port for repairs?"

"Ideally, yeah."

"Good. We'll head back to Watchtower. I'm sure Admiral Kostecki will be more than happy to help out."

"You can't be serious!" Althaus wailed. "If what your saying is true, they planted that beacon so the McKinleys could find us."

"They weren't the McKinleys, and that wasn't *The Gallant Trader*. It was a setup, to make it seem like revenge by a disgruntled former employer."

"They wanted us gone." Kevin swiveled around in his chair. "We know too much about everything that happened with Psi-Aion and the Seekers. They didn't want to risk us revealing it even with the nondisclosure agreements."

"Yet you still want to go back there?" Althaus scratched his forehead.

"We weren't destroyed, which means we've suddenly become more valuable alive." Jason stood and walked over to the operations station, studying the damage reports. "And tell me where we'll get all these repairs done this far from civilization?"

Althaus didn't answer.

Jason proceeded over to the helm and put a hand on Kevin's console. "When Aly gives you the go-ahead, set a course."

FOURTEEN

Outpost Watchtower

"Are you ready, Javier?"

Jonathan Avery stared across Outpost Watchtower's operations center at him while he checked over the last of the diagnostics. Their two previous failures gave Javier plenty of information to work with. He hoped the third time would be the charm.

"Flick the switch," he instructed his friend.

The entire Destiny Resonance Telescope team filled the operations center and watched on as Jonathan toggled at the main controls. The transfer from the station directly into the telescope commenced and it immediately surged to eighty percent and then to ninety. It eventually smoothed out and crept all the way to one hundred.

Jonathan's mouth gaped open, and he looked over at Javier and smiled. They didn't speak a word, but both knew what each other were thinking.

But the telescope itself still had to be switched on.

Jonathan ran his sweaty hands over the console, and all the controls lit up. A star chart spanning hundreds of light-years appeared on the large wall monitor on the rear bulkhead of the operations center. "We're operational!"

Everyone broke out into applause and raucous yelling. Javier stood back and let the Destiny team enjoy their moment. He understood what elation felt like after so many years of torture.

With the shaking of hands and enthusiastic hugs spreading like wildfire, Jonathan approached Javier's side. "Thank you for your assistance. We couldn't have done this without you."

"You flatter me too much," Javier said. "I'm just happy to help."

Jonathan slapped him on the back and one of his assistants gave the pair a glass each. Before they knew it, champagne was consumed by everyone throughout the deck.

The crew lounge of Outpost Watchtower looked like an elephant had run through it. The team from the Destiny Resonance Telescope had hijacked it to celebrate their achievement, and Captain Lang spared no expense, giving them full access to the bar so they could let their hair down.

Javier imagined the outpost's CO just wanted to get the boisterous civilians out of his command center so his station might return to some normality. Regardless, it was a nice gesture on his part. At the end of the night, there were still a few groups of the younger men and women drinking wine and other harsher spirits, while others nursed their heads at the various tables. A few even paired up and find their quarters for the evening.

To be young again.

Javier put down the half-empty glass of champagne, which he'd had well enough of, and stood from his barstool. But before he could move to the exit, Mister Caruso stopped him in his tracks.

"Professor, can I have a moment?" the kid slurred out, barely able to stand.

Javier smiled politely. "Sure."

"I thought I'd give you our thanks on behalf of us all. No one in their wildest dreams believed we'd have the pleasure of working with such a..." Caruso trailed off, trying to find the word. "Ah, genius."

"That's quite all right, Mister Caruso." Javier attempted to move toward the door.

"I wonder if there's a chance you might put a good word in for me when you get back to the Institute. I'd love to come and work with you."

Javier had been impressed with the young man's demeanor when they'd worked together on the telescope. But TIAS only took the best and brightest, and he was hardly in any state for an interview at that moment.

"Avery to Professor Petit."

"I'll need to get that." Javier nudged past Caruso and pressed in the intercom on the terminal beside the door. "This is Petit."

"Javier, I thought you might like to listen to the first sounds we picked up on the telescope."

"I'll be right up." He turned off the intercom and tried to slink away from Caruso. Instead, the younger man followed Javier all the way to the operations center, babbling incoherently the whole time.

Jonathan was standing by the main console with one of his junior assistants when they entered. He looked up and smiled at Javier and frowned at his sloshed subordinate.

"Listen to this, Javier. We've picked up the siren song of a yellow star four hundred light-years away."

Siren songs were a nickname for the 'music' stars made when they were accumulating new material at their surface. The sounds themselves were at such a high frequency only the best hardware detected them.

Jonathan nodded at his assistant, and throughout the operations center the ethereal whispers of the far-away sun played out over the speakers. Javier closed his eyelids and imagined he was sitting in a theatre house somewhere back on Earth listening to a grand opera.

"It sounds like Beethoven."

Javier opened his eyes and turned to the drunkard behind him who'd made the comment. Jonathan was about to say something, but Javier stopped him.

"What do you mean it sounds like Beethoven, Mister Caruso?"

Caruso looked at him as if he were deaf and gestured toward the console. "May I?"

Jonathan told his assistant to relent his chair, and Caruso sat. His hands ran over the station like a man on a mission.

"Because of the distance the siren songs have traveled, they're riddled with interference," Caruso began, all of sudden doing well to be comprehendible. "But if we filter it out and compensate for the dispersion, we get this."

He played it again. Jonathan raised a brow, not understanding, but Javier heard it.

"Mister Caruso, can you speed that up?" he asked him.

Caruso nodded and keyed in the commands. He leaned back in his chair and sung the notes along with the sounds. "B, B, C, D, D, C, B, A, G, G, A, B, B, A, A."

Jonathan's mouth dropped. "Jesus Christ, that's the *Ode to Joy*."

Javier turned to the closest Watchtower officer. "Ensign, I need a pod to the *Repulse* now."

"Why, Javier?" Jonathan asked him. "What does this mean?"

"Something I didn't believe possible."

UECS Repulse

Javier hurried up the corridor of the *Repulse*, struggling to contain his excitement. He couldn't remember the last time he'd moved so fast.

Around a corner, he spotted two guards at each side of the door to Susan's room. Before he said anything, one of them put up a halting hand.

"I'm sorry, Professor, but Doctor Tai already has a visitor."

"Yes, I realize who's in there." He handed the guard a data tablet. "I have Admiral Kostecki's permission."

The guard checked the orders and nodded. He and his colleague stepped aside, and Javier pushed the door in. The lights were dim, and at the center of the room the tall figure of Kione stood over Susan's bed. Javier moved closer, doing his best not to disturb them.

In the light's gleam from an adjacent monitor, there appeared to be a small injection vial in Kione's hand.

No, he didn't...

He grabbed it from the alien and glanced down at it.

"It's not cyclotrol, if that's what you're thinking," Kione whispered.

"Lovacine?" Javier furrowed his brow.

"It's a sleeping drug," Kione said.

Susan's eyes drifted into slumber ever so slowly.

"I couldn't kill her, Professor."

Javier breathed out a sigh of relief. "How did you come to the decision?"

Kione attempted to find the words, until he finally

opened his mouth. "I guess I've spent too long amongst humans."

Javier smiled and sat by Susan's side. He put his hand on hers, and her eyes closed fully. He wasn't sure whether she'd understand him or not, but he had to tell her the news.

"He's alive, Susan. Nicolas is alive."

FIFTEEN

Outpost Watchtower

The rear access ramp of the *Argo* opened, and Jason walked onto the hangar deck of Outpost Watchtower. Professor Petit waited for him at the bottom along with an old friend.

"David Ortega." Jason shook his hand. "You've got old."

"Haven't we all?"

"Lucky for us."

"Is it true?" Aly asked Petit as she Kevin and Althaus came down the ramp.

The professor nodded and gestured toward the door. Everyone followed him into the corridor and then into an elevator. At the command level they arrived at the outpost's operations center. They gathered around Petit at one of the consoles, and he ran his hands over it.

The speakers came alive with music and the sound

echoed eerily, bouncing from one bulkhead to the next. The tune was unmistakable.

"The Ode to Joy," Jason whispered, with the realization Marquez wasn't dead, and with any luck, neither was Tyler. He didn't know how or why. At that moment, he didn't care. "Where does the message emanate from?"

Ortega pointed at the star chart on the main monitor. The Psi-Aion system was at the center of the map, and beyond it was the point of the signal. "It's coming from the GP-34 system. It's situated in the middle of the Horizon Cluster—a far-flung group of stars four hundred and nine light-years away from Outpost Watchtower."

Jason's heart sank. "That's over a one hundred light-years farther than Psi-Aion. How have they been able to send a transmission so quickly? Shouldn't it take years to receive a message from that far away?"

"It would seem they've somehow come across technology that sends audio much more rapidly than anything we can fathom," Petit said.

"More to the point, how did they survive the weapon ship's shock wave?" Althaus asked skeptically.

"We still don't understand a lot about the power contained within the sphere. I assumed the shock wave enveloped and disintegrated them. Instead, it looks like it propelled the *Maybelle* across space."

Aly stepped toward the wall monitor. "The question is, how can we rescue them if they're that far away?"

The room fell silent.

While Jason was glad to find out his brother was hopefully alive, he couldn't help feel more hopeless than he had before.

"Hey, everyone, the president is about to speak!" said one of Outpost Watchtower's junior officers, interrupting them. Ortega walked over to him and nodded. The star chart disappeared and was promptly replaced with the image of President Jarret sitting behind his desk.

Caput Mundi House - Istanbul, Earth

Glendon Jarret had been used to the limelight since his days in school. But even he feared staring down the lens of the camera knowing how important the next few minutes would be. He steepled his fingers on the desk in front of him and looked toward the camera with the most forthright expression he could muster.

"People of the commonwealth. It's with a heavy heart that I bring you news of an attack on our sovereignty. On the twenty-second of October, a decium ore mining facility on the edge of known territory was attacked by a malevolent new enemy. All lives on Orion V, including the valiant fighting men and women of the *UECS Vanguard,* were lost. It has come to my administration's attention in the last few days that this barbaric strike resulted from our adversary's desire for a relic discovered beneath the surface of Orion V. As many of you have seen by now, Marissa Caldwell of the *Martian Tri-*

bune has released details regarding this incident. To those families whose lives were rocked by this attack, we apologize. We had every intention of releasing the information ourselves, but not before we completed the proper investigations.

"To the mothers, fathers, brothers, sisters, and children we now say, all the commonwealth mourns with you. As President of the United Earth Commonwealth, I will do everything within my power to bring justice to those who orchestrated this crime. Those who have watched Miss Caldwell's report no doubt have questions about the extraterrestrial employed in our study of the ancient relic on Orion V. I could blame the many presidents and many administrations in office before me for continuing to cover up the proof that we're no longer alone in the universe. But I'm a bigger man than that. We share that responsibility equally. It will be this president's pledge to right that wrong.

"We've entered a new age. A new dawn. Humanity is no longer the center of the universe. And, unfortunately, from what we've seen already, those out there aren't as friendly as we'd have liked. My promise to you is that as President of the United Earth Commonwealth, I will do exactly what I did during the war. I will protect our sovereignty, our culture, and way of life…"

Outpost Watchtower

"I can't listen to that anymore."

It'd been the third time Jason had watched Jarret's

speech, and it hadn't got any less pathetic with each additional airing. It wasn't so much of an announcement but instead an election pitch. He hoped the people of the commonwealth would see through it, but he knew how democracy worked.

The barman turned it off, and Ortega swiveled around on the stool beside him. "And to think you voted for him."

Jason didn't need reminding. "From memory, so did you."

"Well, he promised a swift end to the war. To be fair, he kept his vow."

"Yes, but by pressing the button." Jason gulped his lager. "And right as it seems the people have finally woken up to him after all these years, fear is once again being stoked to keep the sheep in line." He shook his head. "I hate that I've played a part in that."

Footsteps sounded from the door of the near-empty crew lounge, and Commander Hariri stepped over the threshold.

"Mister Cassidy. Admiral Kostecki would like to see you," she said.

"I've been looking forward to this." Jason drained the rest of his beer and put a hand on Ortega's shoulder. "Thanks for the drink."

SIXTEEN

UECS Repulse

Commander Hariri directed Jason to sit in Kostecki's empty office, and told him the admiral would be with him shortly.

He waited, and he waited. Jason swore an entire hour passed until the *Repulse's* CO finally turned up. Then without so much as an apology, he walked in, passing Jason by and taking a seat on his chair on the opposite side of the desk. Jason realized it was the admiral's way of putting himself in the power position. Unlike last time, though, Jason held the upper hand.

"I suppose you got caught up watching the news?" he asked the admiral.

Kostecki glared at him.

"Astounding, wasn't it? Imagine if that report hadn't broken when it did." Jason pulled out a fist-sized apparatus and placed it on the desk between them. "I guess my crew and I would be floating around the bottom of Verada IV by now if that were the case."

The admiral's eyes darted down at the homing device Aly had yanked from the *Argo's* engine and looked back up at him with a face of stone. While Jason didn't believe Kostecki had anything to do with their near deaths, he was responsible following an order to place the beacon on their ship in the first place.

"Are you done, Mister Cassidy?" the admiral finally said.

Jason wondered whether to continue making his point or not. Once upon a time he might have. But perhaps he'd grown a little wiser as he'd got older. "I guess I am."

"I've received word from the Admiral of Fleet Operations. With what has transpired in recent days, the CDF, along with the Ministry of Defense, are looking for some extra help."

"Extra help?"

"Command have instructed me to ask you to rejoin the service."

Everything around Jason seemed to stop. He remembered the day he'd got his marching orders as if they were yesterday. His life had been the CDF, and to have it stripped away had destroyed him.

"Your dishonorable discharge would be overturned, and you'd be reinstated with the rank of full commander," Kostecki said, shifting uncomfortably in his chair.

Suddenly Jason had gone from being completely dispensable to being a sought-after commodity. So much so they'd given him a promotion. Since the moment he'd left, he'd always wanted to return. But now when he thought about it, he wasn't so sure anymore.

These are the same people who signed my death warrant.

"They've also authorized me to green light repairs for your cargo ship should you require them." Kostecki slid over a data tablet with a timetable of the repairs.

"With or without the homing beacon this time?" Jason asked sarcastically.

"I'll ensure my team leave the *Argo* in as near original condition as possible."

Jason did his best to hide his irritation. "I'll let my crew know to expect your help."

"Good." Kostecki took back the data tablet. "Now we come to the matter of your decision."

Jason didn't know what to say. It wasn't something he could take lightly. He had so many options for the first time in what seemed like forever. But everything had changed now that Tyler might be alive. "I'll need to think about it."

Kostecki nodded. "Don't take too long."

Jason pushed the door open to the sight of Doctor Tai sitting in her mobility chair with Beethoven's *Number Nine* playing over the speakers. She was a shell of her former self.

Professor Petit peered up, while helping her get

around the room in her chair. "Mister Cassidy."

Jason nodded and smiled at Tai. "It's good to see you, Doctor."

She put her hand on Petit's arm. "I need a word with Mister Cassidy in private?"

Petit left the ward, closing the door behind him. Jason took a seat beside her unoccupied bed while she wheeled her chair toward him.

"The professor told me everything that happened," she began. "You got very lucky."

"Sometimes you make your own luck."

"Indeed. How did you do it?"

Jason grinned.

"Come on, no doubt even the brass at the CDF figure you somehow got word out before the *Argo* was intercepted by the *Repulse,* after we left the trans-space corridor."

"A little trick I picked up during the war." Jason knew Tai had served in the CDF before her time with TIAS so she grasped how the world worked. "Before we sent out our original call to Outpost Watchtower, I left a worm in a nearby comm satellite."

"A worm?"

Jason nodded. "It's a term for a data packet in limbo. I wasn't sure if we'd need it, but after we called Watchtower and the *Repulse* blocked all our outgoing commlinks, I knew we did. We'd be interrogated, and at that stage I wasn't sure what that'd mean for us, but I realized it mightn't be good. Luckily, I transmitted a low frequency beam, one much too low to be blocked by the jamming field or to be picked up by scanners, but sufficient enough to activate my worm."

"And you sent it off to the *Martian Tribune*?"

"An old friend works there. It may have taken a while to get to her, but it did just in time."

"Almost genius."

"Enough to save our lives at least. If they'd destroyed us with that story out, people would've asked questions. It seems those with their finger on the trigger realized that."

She nodded. "You're like a cat, Mister Cassidy. How many lives do you have left?"

Jason laughed, and they sat in silence for several moments until it was his turn to put the blowtorch on her. "Professor Petit told me everything that happened with you."

"He's such a gossip." Tai frowned. "I must have a word with him."

He looked at her with concern. "Are you okay?"

She chuckled. "If you're asking me if I've got any more suicidal tendencies? No, I don't. Since hearing this..." She gestured to the music playing over the speakers. "My priorities have changed. I'm sure you feel the same."

Jason nodded.

"I want you to promise me, Mister Cassidy, that you'll do everything in your power to rescue them."

Jason wasn't sure how to begin planning something of such magnitude, but somehow, he'd make sure to figure it out. "Don't worry, I'll bring them home."

SEVENTEEN

"They told me you were the best. The best of the best. The most elite recruits the academy had to offer!"

Commander Jason Cassidy stood at the front of the situation room glaring at his twelve cadets while they all did their best not to make eye contact with him.

He picked up a data tablet and placed it on the lectern. "Hayes, during the Bryson Maneuver, you were too late punching your thrusters on the starboard roll. Newcombe, you were too early. And, Delesio, don't even get me started on that miserable excuse of an evasive maneuver you pulled during the simulated attack. You not only would've got yourself killed, but your gunner as well."

"But, Commander—"

"Did I say you could speak, Cadet?"

Delesio buttoned his lips.

Jason shook his head and frisbeed the tablet over to him. "In my day, my instructor would've grounded me if I'd made as many mistakes as you did."

Not that 'my day' was that long ago.

He sometimes had to remind himself at the beginning of the Earth-Centauri War, he was only a raw ensign out of the academy. One thrust into the chaos of all-out conflict. Now, only a few years later, he held the rank of Lieutenant Commander and was instructing the pilots of the future.

"If any of you were recruited during those years, the Centauri would've blown you to pieces in your first skirmish. You're all very lucky it's peacetime." He narrowed his eyes and stared at every one of his students. "I don't know how the hell I can sign you all off on simulation work in the asteroid field with these kind of results."

No one made a peep.

"Get out of my sight. Report back here at oh-seven hundred tomorrow morning."

The cadets turned on their heels and briskly filed out.

From beneath the lectern, Jason plucked out a small flask of bourbon and took a few nips. He closed his eyes as the soothing liquor ran down his throat.

"Bit hard on them, don't you think?"

Jason opened his eyes and quickly stashed the drink out of sight. He spun around to find Chief Lin standing by the door.

Jason frowned. "They didn't treat me with kid gloves when I went through the academy."

"No, but you were a good pilot before you got there."

"All the more reason to fire a rocket up these kids'

asses. I remember when I came here as a cadet to do my first live high-speed maneuvers. It was brutal. If you stuffed up even once, you were dead. And so were the people around you."

Lin walked in and took a seat at a chair in front of the lectern. He regarded Jason with his harsh but thoughtful eyes. "I understand. I'm just saying that sometimes a lighter touch might work just as well. They need someone to show them how it's done. You're constantly blasting them from pillar to post."

When Jason left the *Raptor* at the end of the war to take up a position as a flight instructor at the Olbers Training Station, he was amazed when Lin requested a transfer to the same facility. The chief maintained he did it to be closer to home as he crept ever nearer to retirement, but Jason often wondered if it had anything to do with keeping an eye on him after Christian Nash's death. Regardless, he enjoyed listening to his kernels of wisdom. "I'll take it under advisement."

"Good." Lin smiled. "Cards tonight? There'll be a few of us down in the rec later."

"I think I'll have a quiet night in."

"You always have quiet nights in these days." Lin clenched his hands into fists. "Come on, don't you want to take down everyone like you used to on the *Raptor*?"

"Another night perhaps," Jason lied. While he'd once enjoyed off-duty time with his colleagues, things were different now.

"If you change your mind, you know where to find

us." Lin exited the situation room, and closed the door behind him.

Jason unscrewed the top of his bourbon and guzzled it down.

You son of a bitch, Nash.

Nash's pod exploded again and again and the swirling gases of the nebula burst into a great plume of color. The image haunted Jason whenever he shut his eyes.

He stumbled down the long corridor of the station, assuming it was well past midnight. There was no one anywhere. His cadets were hopefully asleep.

Someone has to show them how it's done.

He rounded the corner and entered the large doors onto the station's hangar deck where rows of pods and fighters sat. He shook off the memory of Nash's pod blowing up and marched toward one of the fighters.

"Commander?"

Jason turned to a hangar deck mechanic standing behind him. *McConnell? McGinnis? McGreevy? Yeah, that sounds right.*

"Mister McGreevy, you're up late," Jason said to him, seeing three of the young man in his intoxicated state.

"It's Smith, sir, and I was about to finish up." The deck jockey eyed him. "What are you doing here?"

"I..." Jason was too drunk to lie. "I'm taking this

fighter out for a spin."

"Uh, I can't allow that."

Jason chuckled. "You realize I'm about a dozen rungs above you in the chain of command?"

"Yes, sir, but you have no authorization to take that bird out. Not at this time of the night, and certainly not in your condition."

He's got balls, I'll give him that.

Jason stepped toward him. "You know, you're probably right." He placed his arm around the young man's shoulders, and they walked to the door.

Noticing the flight suit locker out the corner of his eye, he put Smith in a headlock and threw him in it, sealing him inside with no escape. The mechanic pounded away on the other side of the door, yelling at the top of his lungs.

Jason ignored him and suited up.

Phew! That was close.

An asteroid flew past Jason's cockpit, followed by two more.

Or were they all the same one?

Even though he was drunk off his ass and the controls were too bright for his eyes, he was still alive.

If I can do it, so can they.

He barrel-rolled around a pair of asteroids and nose-dived over another.

The fighter shuddered, and he spun, making contact

with a tiny meteorite. With a deft touch, he fired the port thrusters and leveled it off.

I think I've made my point.

He plotted a course from the field, punching a hole through the middle of a trio of erratic asteroids. When he was in the clear, he squinted at two shapes ahead. They appeared as a pair of bogeys on the scanners.

"Commander Cassidy, power down your engines," the call came over the commlink. *"Prepare for towing maneuvers."*

"I can get back there on my own," he snipped at the other pilot, who'd obviously been sent out to bring him in. "Just lead the way."

They seemed in no mood for an argument. One dropped its grapple cable and latched on to Jason's fighter, jolting him in his seat.

I guess nothing else to do now but enjoy the ride.

The stroll to the captain's office was much less enjoyable. Four of the station's security goons met him in the hangar deck and dragged him through the corridors of the station, placing him down in a chair in front of Captain Kaufman's desk.

His CO's hair was flat at the back and stuck up at the front, and his uniform was covered in creases. "Explain yourself, Commander," he said with a yawn. "I hope there's a good story for your little escapade."

Jason cleared his throat. "I guess I was trying to

show my cadets how good they must be before I give them the tick of approval."

"Really? Because it's oh-three hundred in the morning, and all your cadets are in bed."

"I assumed it was recorded by the station's scanners."

"You got that right. Along with the amount of alcohol in your system."

The security guard handed Kaufman a medical scanner.

The captain checked it and threw it down in disgust. "Damn it, Cassidy, I can smell it from here!" He sat and placed his hands together. "What's this really about?"

Jason closed his eyes again, greeted with the images haunting him. He shied away from Kaufman.

"I need something to work with here. The instructor of the finest flight cadets in the fleet has just gone AWOL on a bender, in millions of credits worth of hardware, and nearly got himself killed. HQ will ask questions. What am I supposed to tell them?"

Jason stared at Kaufman, keeping his mouth firmly shut.

"Very well." Kaufman sighed. "Effective immediately, you're grounded and stripped of your position for an indefinite period, pending an investigation."

Jason jumped out of his seat, sending his chair flying backward. "No!"

Kaufman stood and walked around his desk to face him. "You leave me no choice, Commander."

Without thinking, Jason swung his fist through the air. It connected with Kaufman's jaw, throwing him onto his desk.

The guards beside Jason rushed him, seizing each of his arms. He struggled at first but finally relented.

What have I done?

Kaufman touched the growing lump on his face. "Put him in the brig!"

"Aly to Jason."

"Aly to Jason. Come in," she repeated.

Jason opened his eyes and stared up at the ceiling of his quarters. He pushed away his sheets and dabbed the perspiration from his head. He'd woken from the same dream he'd had on and off since returning to Earth from Outpost Watchtower. The same nightmare that began after leaving the *Raptor* to attempt a new start in the service. One in which he ultimately failed. And just like all the other times, he'd woken in a pool of his own sweat.

He threw his feet down and pushed on the intercom beside his bed. "This is Jason. What is it Aly?"

"I just thought you'd like to know that we've entered the Sol system. We'll be at Earth within in the next few hours."

"Thank you, Aly." A lump formed in his throat and he stood, staring out the viewport. Soon he'd be back where it all started.

I wonder if they'll accept me?

EIGHTEEN

Caput Mundi House - Istanbul, Earth

"Congratulations, Mister Cassidy."

Jason bowed, and President Jarret placed a medal around his neck. The commander in chief smiled and shook his hand, raising it to the audience.

If Jason didn't know that it was Jarret, who, had made the call to execute him, he probably would've felt more comfortable. But it was hard to forget how close he and the crew of the *Argo* had been from being blasted into pieces at the great gas giant of Verada IV.

Jason put on the face expected of him and acted nice for the president, the cameras, and the hundreds of people sitting around the tables in the grand banquet hall. Deep inside, however, there was a hollowness. Jarret was only using him and the others as a publicity stunt.

When knowledge had come out about Orion V, Psi-Aion, the Seekers, the sphere, and everything else, the president had no alternative but to fawn over the crew of the *Argo*. They were heroes. And were treated accordingly. It was the only thing getting Jason through the horrid event.

"The Pernov Medal is the highest civilian honor," Jarret announced to the crowd. "The fine men and women here are the definition of what Alexei Pernov stood for. If it weren't for them, I fear what Earth would now be facing." He put a hand on Jason's shoulder. "You see, it's people like Mister Cassidy who got us through our most recent conflict. This man fought bravely from the day he stepped out of the academy, and no doubt his training in our fine institution aided him in defeating the Seekers."

Jason wanted to vomit at the nauseating claptrap.

"Luckily for us, he's agreed to rejoin the CDF in service to Earth and the commonwealth," the Jarret continued, as applause broke out around the banquet hall. Jarret put his hand down and walked to the front of the stage. "Without people like Jason Cassidy, I fear the coming age we enter. Years after slaying one enemy, it appears we must now face another."

The spherical autonomous camera hovered a meter away from him, and he stared down its lens. "We need to make our minds up. Do we go into the trenches with the soldiers who won us our last war or do we risk destroying everything we've rebuilt?"

Earth was well and truly in election mode when Jason had stepped off the *Repulse*. The crew of the *Argo* quickly became pawns to be paraded around.

Jason glanced at his comrades beside him on the stage. Kevin Rycroft looked dapper in his tuxedo, while Althaus struggled to fit in the one he'd shoehorned himself into.

How his head fits out of that neck hole would baffle most physics scientists.

Aly was like a fairy princess in her shoulder-exposing dress. It was much nicer than her filthy overalls. And Professor Petit appeared a seasoned pro in his suit.

Jason wished Doctor Tai had decided to come but understood when she'd declined. It was the other person missing that rankled him the most. He imagined his brother standing next to Aly, wishing they could all be together again.

It'd been a whirlwind six months returning to Earth, with their hopes high after discovering that Captain Marquez and, with any luck, Tyler Cassidy, weren't as dead as they'd first thought. How they were alive was still a mystery, but one Jason could live with for the time being. What was difficult to contend with was the phenomenal distance between them.

"Can we go yet?" Althaus glared at him.

"Come on, you look good in that penguin suit. It shows off all your sleek lines."

Althaus harrumphed.

"I'm sorry, I didn't realize it'd be this bad," Jason said to Kevin.

"It's nice to dress up for a change. Especially with all that's happened." Kevin gazed over at Aly. "And to see my little girl so elegant. It's worth it just for that."

After the reception was over and everyone feasted on the dinner served, Jason walked onto the presidential grounds to get some air. The greenness of the freshly cut lawns and prize-winning flowers were out of place in the center of the great metropolis once known as Constantinople.

"Did you tire of all the lavish praise?"

"Ha-ha." Jason glanced up at Aly stepping down the stairs in her high heels. He found her attempts at standing upright quite amusing. He couldn't remember the last time he'd seen her wear a pair, if ever. "Maybe you should've kept your training wheels on."

"Oh, shut up." She sat next to him on one of the lower steps and gazed out at the brightly lit skyscrapers. "While I appreciate the beauty here, it still doesn't compare to the sights we've seen aboard the *Argo*."

Jason chuckled. "I've already listened to enough of Jarret pitching for his next term in office, I don't need to hear yours about keeping me on the ship."

After their little moment on the *Argo* six months earlier, where her angry outburst had turned into a kiss, she'd given him some leeway on the subject.

"You can't blame me for trying," she said.

"I guess not." He playfully poked at her earrings sparkling in the moonlight.

"When will you be recalled?" she asked.

"I'm to report to HQ in a few days."

"Are you worried?"

"No, but I don't know what to expect. With everything that happened with my dishonorable discharge, I never thought I'd be in the service again. I suppose I got lucky."

"And working under Jarret?"

"I'm not working for Jarret. I'll be in the defense force."

"Correct me if I'm mistaken, but don't they take their orders from the president."

He frowned. "Sometimes you do what you need to do."

Aly gave him a knowing look. One he'd gotten sick of on their return journey. "You didn't have to accept."

"We've discussed this. We all agreed that should there be a way to rescue Tyler and Captain Marquez, it's better for me to have a voice in the matter, and that's more likely in the CDF."

"And how likely do you think that is?"

"You would know more than me."

She chuckled. "They cooped up Professor Petit in his quarters on the *Repulse* from the day we left Outpost Watchtower. They'd have told him not to discuss any of his work on trans-space."

"I guess you're right." Jason frowned. "How's everything with the *Argo*?"

"We're docked at Highfield Station and due to receive our first load of cargo soon. All we need now is a captain."

It was a decision Jason had put on hold during their journey back from Watchtower, much to Althaus's chagrin. He hoped the choice he made wouldn't create friction between them. "Believe it or not, I've decided on the ideal candidate."

She opened her mouth and covered it in mock horror.

Jason smiled. "It's you, Aly."

She furrowed her brow, and blinked a few more times than normal. "Me? I..."

Considering Althaus and Kevin were the only two in the running, or at least so they thought, he understood her shock. And loved every second of it.

"I don't know what to say," she said.

"Say yes."

"But—"

Jason put a hand on hers. "Aly, as much as I love your dad and tolerate Althaus, they've had their time. This is a chance for a new generation to take the reins. I'm sure it's what Tyler and my father would've wanted."

A tear ran down her cheek.

"And no one knows the ins and outs of the *Argo* like you."

Aly threw her arms around him. "You realize Althaus will flip when he finds out?"

"Let him flip. Your first command decision can be to decide what to do about any insubordination. May I suggest spacing him out the airlock?"

They both laughed and stared out at the view beyond, knowing it would be a very long time before they got to share a moment like it again.

NINETEEN

Ministry of Defense Building - Istanbul, Earth

"A drink, Professor?"

Javier Petit waved away the offer from Mister Takashi. He and the minister had known each for some time with all the work Javier had done at the Tokyo Institute of Advanced Sciences for the Ministry of Defense. But there seemed to be something Takashi could never understand about him. Javier was fanatical regarding time. Specifically, his own. The last thing he wanted to do was get stuck in a stuffy office when his work awaited.

Takashi put the bottle away inside his liquor cabinet and took a seat behind his desk. "Well, let's get down to business then." He pulled out a data tablet from his drawer. "Since your debriefing six months ago at Outpost Watchtower, you can imagine how excited the president was in regard to the discovery of trans-space."

"That's understandable," Javier said.

"It makes our conventional FTL drive resemble something from the Middle Ages."

"I can't argue with that."

"The question for you, Professor, is after six months of continued study, is it viable? You replicated it to bring the *Argo* home from the Psi-Aion system and—"

"That's incorrect." Javier wondered if he'd even read his report. "I expanded an already existing trans-space vortex, using the Iota particles salvaged from the *Argo*'s engine. It was crude but effective."

"So, what's the difference?"

Spoken like a true bureaucrat.

"Creating a stable trans-space vortex from scratch right now is a technological impossibility."

"If there's anyone this administration trusts in changing that, it's you," Takashi said, confidently.

"Well, I'm not so sure about that."

"You're too modest, Professor."

Javier chuckled. He'd not heard anyone say that of him before. He knew enough to realize he was just being buttered up.

Takashi stood and walked over to his bookcase to wipe away some dust that was obviously annoying him. "You must have made progress in the last six months while aboard the *Repulse*."

"I've put together a lot of ideas. But this isn't something solved overnight. It took decades to develop a working FTL drive after the first reserves of tritonium were tapped."

"What do you need? President Jarret wants to see

trans-space realized. You can have all the resources you want." Takashi slid his data tablet over to Javier. "Make a list."

Javier stared down at the empty screen and smiled. There was nothing he liked more than a blank check.

Miami, Earth

Jason couldn't remember the last time he'd had sweaty palms. As he looked out onto the bustling Miami Beach promenade from the confines of the quaint little coffee shop, he considered getting up and leaving. He never liked the idea of being stood up.

No, I owe her more than that.

A waitress approached him. "Would you like another drink?"

Jason peered into his empty cup. "Uh—"

"Yes, he will."

Jason craned his neck past the waitress, and on the backdrop of the beach, Marissa Caldwell strolled toward him as if she'd emerged from the sea.

"I'll have a double-strength latte," she said.

"You always liked the heavy stuff, didn't you?"

The waitress put the order on her data tablet and walked off.

Marissa took her seat at the small table, opposite Jason. "I never seem to get a break, so I constantly caffeinate," she told him. "I'm sorry I'm late."

Jason basked in her beauty with the sunlight glistening off the water behind her. "So, you've still got a job then?"

"I didn't think I would after releasing your story. While it pissed of my editor royally, she couldn't bring herself to fire the person who broke the biggest news story of the century. And since I've been at the forefront of all the follow-up pieces, the *Martian Tribune's* sales have soared."

"Fortune favors the bold sometimes. I guess all those dreams you once had have been fulfilled."

The waitress came back with their coffees and placed them down on the table.

Marissa raised her cup. "And to think it was you who got me there."

"Ironic, isn't it?" Jason sipped at his long black. "It was all worth it to save my crew. Thank you, Marissa."

She shook him off. "Please, Jason—"

"Seriously, it must have been hard releasing that information. There was every chance it might've been fake and—"

"We had bad times, but I would never believe you'd do anything to jeopardize my career." She winked. "We had far too many good times for that."

That we did.

"So, how's Mars treating you?" Jason asked. "I never imagined you'd move away from Earth."

"You go to where the work is. I got opportunities with the local North American rags. Then I wrote a piece on the leadership of the Centauri rebellion, and it caught the *Tribune's* eye. I packed up my life and made my way to Holden City. I guess you could say I'm stuck there now."

"Oh?"

"Hmm?" Marissa put down her cup. "Uh, I'm involved."

"Oh." A tingling of jealousy fluttered inside Jason. He did his best not to let it show. "What's his name?"

"Marcus."

Sounds like a jerk.

"I'm sure he's a really nice guy."

"His family were among the first founders of Mars," Marissa said. "He owns a tech company that essentially runs itself."

"Lucky for some." Jason didn't mean it to sound sarcastic. "I'm glad you're happy."

"So, what about you?" She smiled. "Is there someone special in Jason Cassidy's life?"

"I haven't exactly had a chance to hold a relationship down."

"And to think once upon a time you were so good at multitasking. If you didn't have at least three on the go at once—"

"I liked a challenge. So did you if memory serves," he joked.

"You were certainly a challenge."

They both laughed.

Marissa finished up her latte and placed it down. "I'm sorry but I must run."

"Already?"

"My work is never done. However, there is one thing I need to ask before I go."

"So, there's another reason you wanted to see me?" Jason feigned shock.

"I'd like to interview you."

"Ah. That might be difficult. I'm returning to the service. It'll be up to them, and they're not usually too fond of—"

"I've already been in contact with Admiral Mueller's office, and she's given me the green light for a tell-all interview."

"Oh." Jason shrugged. "Well, I guess I have little choice."

"We'll talk and organize a date." She stood and blushed, realizing what she'd said. "A date for the time of the interview, I mean."

Jason smirked. "Until then..."

She walked back toward the beach and Jason felt at his chest, wondering why his heart was thumping so hard. He hoped it wasn't what he thought it was.

TWENTY

Tokyo Institute of Advanced Sciences - Tokyo, Earth

With everything that had happened after leaving Earth on the *Vanguard* and being whisked away to Psi-Aion, Susan Tai couldn't believe it'd been a year since she'd left TIAS.

The lobby of the great building was a hive of activity. Everyone seemed to be in a hurry.

All except me.

While the last six months aboard the *Repulse* had given her time to get used to her specialized wheelchair, after a lifetime of full mobility, it was something she still struggled with. At the security entrance of the lobby, people either gawked at her as if she were a horrible mutant, or completely ignored her like she wasn't even there.

"Excuse me?" Susan said to the person manning the gate. "Where's Charlie?"

"He's retired." His successor put out a small data

tablet, which Susan placed her hand on. It recognized her clearance, and the barrier ahead opened.

"You can go through, Doctor Tai," the new guard said blankly, returning to a conversation with her colleague.

Susan took a last glance at the lifeless automaton of a person who'd replaced the gentle old man and made her way to the central elevators. She entered one, and after a quick ride downward, arrived on the Green Level. The doors swooshed open, revealing her old stomping ground. At least a dozen of her staff worked away at their computers while she directed her chair out of the elevator.

There were a few new faces, but the rest all looked familiar. One stood, recognizing her. Followed by another, until everyone else came over to her with wide smiles. In their eyes, however, Susan only saw pity.

"Doctor!"

Brendan O'Malley moved through the small crowd. Her trusty right-hand man's grin lit up the room. She could tell he wanted to hug her but wasn't exactly sure how.

"It's good to see you again, Brendan." Tai raised her hand and shook his. "And everyone else," she said to the others. "I hope you've all been hard at work while I was gone."

"We've done what we can." Brendan placed a hand on the back of her chair. "Come through to your office. I promise I didn't change it too much."

He gave the staff a subtle nod to return to their duties, and Susan followed him through to the workspace she'd relinquished to him before leaving for Orion V. True to his word, apart from a few family photos on the desk, little had changed. A warmth filled her heart in the familiar confines.

Brendan sat on the edge of the desk. "You can't believe how glad I am to have you back, Susan."

"Okay, spill the beans." She detected hesitation in his voice. "I might be confined to this chair but I'm a big girl. If they've given you the project, I deserve to know. Though I would've preferred Remy tell me first."

"It's not that." He watched through the window at the others. "Not exactly anyway."

Susan swiveled her head. Her staff were packing up workstations and filing away data tablets into boxes. "Brendan, what the hell is going on?"

"They've shut us down, Susan."

"Shut us down!" She darted her eyes back at him. "Are they letting Kione go?"

With his existence exposed by Marissa Caldwell six months earlier, she'd hoped he'd be able to enter public life. While she had no desire to be out of a job, Kione's happiness was her priority.

"Another team were reassigned to him. We're not sure where he's gone. The Ministry of Defense haven't told us anything."

Susan's elation turned to fear. It was the exact opposite of the news she wanted to hear. At least if he was at TIAS she'd be able to protect him, but now...

Goddamn it!

Unknown Facility

Brightness washed over Kione, and a tingling warmth radiated through his icy body.

"Can you hear me?"

His eyes struggled with the light above and the room blurred into the image of a hundred stars. He took a few moments to gather his bearings until his vision finally improved.

A face stared down at him. One he'd never seen before. His hair was jet-black and the lines of his brow harsh. The man gave Kione a hand, and he heaved his stiff body from the cryogenic chamber. It'd been his second trip in one and it hadn't been any more pleasant than the first.

Kione hoped to come back to Earth on the *Repulse* without the need to travel in his icy coffin, since the public were now aware of his existence. Due to 'security reasons' he'd been put in, regardless.

"Who are you?" Kione asked.

"My name's Doctor Charles Whitlowe."

Kione glanced behind him at the pair of armed guards dressed in black. "And where's Doctor Tai?"

"Doctor Tai is no longer the director of the project into your study."

He peered around the dimly lit confines. "Am I to gather I'm also not at the Institute either?"

"You are correct."

"Why?"

"The Ministry of Defense thought it prudent to put

you under the care of someone other than the doctor and her team at TIAS." Whitlowe pulled out a small medical scanner and waved it over him. "After all, they've had you to themselves for over thirty years. With what happened on your excursion and the contact you had with the sphere, they're after a second opinion."

Whitlowe studied the readings on the scanner, seemingly impressed. "Understand, the abilities you gained when you were aboard the Seeker ship have made the Ministry of Defense very curious." He placed the medical scanner away and put his hands behind his back. "I'm not here to disparage the work of my predecessors. I want to build on them. My aim is to use new methods to see if we can bring your newfound powers to the surface again. Is that something that interests you?"

Kione wasn't sure how to answer. While the thought of unlocking his potential fascinated him, he didn't know whether it was a good idea or not. "One has to question your experience—"

Whitlowe put up a reassuring hand. "For six months I've pored over the data the Institute has collated over the decades. While I may not have experience with a member of your species, I have remarkable expertise making living creatures do things they couldn't ever imagine possible."

Kione raised his brow. "In what field have you worked?"

Whitlowe didn't answer. Instead, he smiled and gestured to the door. "Come, let me show you what I can do."

TWENTY-ONE

Cargo Ship Argo

Aly didn't know whether to be excited or nervous. It'd been a strange couple of days since Jason handed the *Argo* over to her. When she'd signed the official documents, it made it that much more real and terrifying. While she was looking forward to the coming months, there was a hollowness inside the ship. With Tyler gone and now Jason back in the service, things just weren't the same.

She'd spent the last few hours in the engine room doing one final inspection, ensuring the old girl was ready for launch, and then helped her father and Althaus load up the last of their consignment of medical supplies. With a toggle of the controls, she dropped the last container on the deck of the *Argo's* cargo bay and placed the hover-lifter in the corner. She then led both men to the bridge where she had to perform her first proper duties as captain.

Aly wasn't always comfortable being the center of attention. The two men before her had so much experience. And she still felt like a kid. Althaus's brooding didn't help matters either. If anything would get her through the next few days, it would be her dad. He'd been beaming with pride ever since she'd told him Jason had given the *Argo* to her.

"Well," Aly began. "I can't remember the last time we actually hauled cargo and got paid good money to do it. When we returned to Earth, we realized we'd be coming into an area of space with a lot of competition." She glanced at Althaus. "Thank you for organizing this contract with Ganymede Station. For eight months we'll eat well and have plenty of coin leftover. We'll likely not see any Seekers either, which is a plus."

Althaus crossed his arms, giving her a grudging nod of appreciation.

"With any luck, by the end of our contract, we'll find more jobs so we can hang around the solar system a little longer," she continued. "If not, we'll do what we've always done and go to where the work is. Our shuttle runs to the Jovian system won't be easy. E-Class cargo ships weren't designed for a three-person crew. Especially one of this age." Aly put her hand on the captain's chair. "I realize I'm the last one we all thought would say this, but at some point, we may have to consider hiring help. I understand if we bring someone aboard it'll eat into our profits but I've learned you sometimes have to spend money to make money. If it brings more work, in this competitive market it can only be good for all of us. Now, I want to get underway by seventeen-hundred hours. Are there any questions?"

Her dad shook his head, and Althaus walked to the hatchway without saying so much as boo.

"He'll come around," her father said to her.

"When? He holds grudges longer than anyone else I've known."

"You are the captain of the ship." He smirked. "You could just fire him."

Aly chuckled. "While there is a certain appeal to that, it may stretch us too thin."

"I'm sure you'll figure something out. Jason wouldn't have given the *Argo* to you otherwise."

"Is that the best advice my most trusted confidant can give me?"

Her dad laughed. "I'll have a few nuggets of wisdom up my sleeve from time to time, but as captain there's a lot you must discover on your own. Like you said before, this won't be easy. But as long as you trust your instincts, you'll do just fine."

He pulled her in for a hug. Just as loving as the ones he'd given her when she was a little girl. "And you know how I know this?"

"How?" she asked.

"Because I raised you and did a superb job of it."

Aly slapped him on the chest. "I can always trust you to turn such a sweet moment into a joke. Get started on the pre-flights, would you?"

He stepped to the helm and mock saluted. "Yes, sir!"

CDF Headquarters - Miami, Earth

While Jason had learned most of his flying skills from Kevin Rycroft, it was Gerald Foster who'd taken his raw talent and honed him into one of the finest pilots the CDF had ever produced.

"Admiral Foster will see you now." An ensign looked across at him from her reception desk in the waiting room.

Jason stood and walked toward the office and pushed the door open. Behind his desk, Admiral Foster was reading a large leather-bound book. Jason saluted, as if he were a cadet again.

"My wife gave me this." Foster held up the publication. "It's an up-to-date history of the Commonwealth Defense Force. There's a lot of names in here. Especially from the war. Some famous. Some infamous. And guess what? There's not a mention anywhere of someone getting away with what you did and being let back into the service. You've done something remarkable returning to these grounds."

"Well, sir, you did once say I was destined for greatness."

"Yes, I did. At ease, Commander." Foster closed the book and stood. "This office's too stuffy for me. Let's go for a walk."

Before Jason knew it, he was strolling the grounds of HQ with the admiral through the beautifully maintained gardens. "It must've been hard for you to see Lieutenant Nash again after all these years."

Jason had trouble getting his friend out of his mind but was becoming more at peace with what had happened the second time around. "I think having seen what they'd done to him, I can find solace now he's properly dead. He wouldn't have wanted to live that way any longer."

"And, Captain Marquez—"

"A person of great honor. In the short time he spent with us on the *Argo,* I understand how he got his reputation."

"You believe this Destiny signal proves he's alive?"

"Yes, sir, I do. I believe both he and my brother are."

Foster smiled. "I hope you're right."

"We owe it to them to do everything in our power to find them."

"Finding them isn't the issue." The admiral raised his brow. "The signal emanates from the Horizon Cluster, four hundred and twenty-nine light-years away. That's over a twenty-year round trip with our current technology. While it's not impossible, it's unlikely anyone would green light such a dangerous and expensive mission."

Jason stopped in the middle of the path. "There is trans-space."

"A technology we're yet to harness."

"But if we do—"

Foster walked over to a bed of beautiful blue and pink flowers and picked one, rolling it around in his hand. "These are big ifs. We have to live in the here and now. You've taken up the offer of coming back into the fold. Some, like me, will welcome you with open arms, knowing what you're capable of. Others won't. And barreling in here like a bull in a china shop will do little to help you with those people."

"I just—"

"Before you put that uniform back on, ask yourself whether you want to be here or not."

Jason had almost forgotten how direct Foster could be. He was harsh but fair. While finding Tyler would always be Jason's number one goal, he understood it wasn't worth lighting fires. Not just yet anyway. He didn't want to get kicked to the curb again, because that wouldn't help him either.

He straightened his back. "I want to be here, Admiral."

"Good. I had a feeling you'd say that." Foster gestured toward the nearby park bench, and they both sat. "With that out of the way, it's time to talk about your assignment." He pulled a small data tablet from his pocket and handed it to Jason. "Admiral Mueller has assigned you to the *UECS Sabre*."

"The *Sabre*? A cruiser." Jason checked over his orders. "First officer?"

"That's right. She's in port at Alpha Station and relaunches in four weeks. You begin duties aboard her in ten days. Use the last of your free time wisely."

"Yes, sir."

Foster grabbed at Jason's beard. "And shave this off. You look like a bum."

TWENTY-TWO

Tokyo Institute of Advanced Sciences - Tokyo, Earth

Javier could never contain his exhilaration on the first day of a new project. While he'd laid the foundation in the last six months on his journey back to Earth, it was back in TIAS where all the hard work would come together.

With help from the Ministry of Defense and the executives at TIAS, he gathered the team he wanted along with some other brilliant minds he didn't expect to have access to. He discovered instantly how important this was to Jarret and his administration with all the resources being given to him.

He peered out at his staff of four hundred in the large briefing hall of the Institute. "Today we begin on a stupendous goal. One when we're successful will put us in the same conversation as Henry Ford, the Wright Brothers, Wernher von Braun, and Mary Poole."

The excited men and women hung on every word.

Javier forgot how amazing it was to deliver one of his famous speeches.

"Being a part of the Mark IV FTL program was a wonderful experience. We took what we knew from the Mark III, refined and enhanced it by using new methods. The Mark V team did much the same when it was their time. But this is very different. We're not here to make the wheel go faster. We're here to reinvent it. Trans-space is real. On my journey through it, I traveled three hundred light-years in a matter of days. By harnessing this technology, we'll open up Earth to the universe. And believe me when I tell you there are wonders out there you won't fathom."

Or nightmares no one will comprehend.

"We've already entered a new age. Now it's up to us to make sure all humanity can share in it."

A clap sounded at the back of the hall. Followed by another. Soon, everyone broke out into wild applause. Javier smiled and stood down from the lectern, while the large gathering of scientists filed out. Professor Felicity Malone, the project's second in charge, approached him at the bottom of the steps.

"How was that?" he asked her.

"You've still got it, Javier. Brought a tear to my eye," she said dryly.

He chuckled. "Can I see the first assignment rosters?"

She handed him a data tablet, and he checked over all the names. The team was split into four main groups. Particle Analysis, who had the job of studying the Iota particle with the intention of replicating it. Medical, who were tasked with shielding passengers from the corridor's debilitating effects. Delivery Systems, who had to figure out how to create an entry and exit vortex. And Navigation, who were assigned with calculating how and where those vortexes would appear.

Javier checked the roster off. Everything seemed in perfect order. He'd begun work on all four areas, now it was up to his people to take what he had and run with it.

He returned the data tablet to Felicity. "Tell Particle Analysis I'll spend my first day with them and rotate between the groups thereafter. You can start with Delivery Systems and do the same."

She nodded. "Anything else?"

He shook his head. "No, I'll be in my office uploading some paperwork. Lunch at one?"

"Sure."

"Good, I'll see you then."

Felicity walked from the hall, and Javier made his way to his office. He sat at his desk and activated the computer. A message awaited him, which he promptly opened.

"Javier, it's Susan. I realize you're busy, but if you've got a moment, I'd like to meet. It's about Kione."

He raised his eyebrows and pressed in the intercom. "Felicity, I'm sorry, I won't be making lunch today."

Tokyo, Earth

Susan's Tokyo apartment wasn't as big as Javier's. But it was comfortable with a nice view of Mount Fuji. It suited her needs, which was now the most important thing.

When Javier walked in the door, his friend's eyes betrayed her feelings. She looked just as she had when she'd asked him to take her life on the *Repulse* six months earlier. He hoped she hadn't regressed.

"What is it, Susan?" he asked.

She invited him inside, and he took a seat across from her on the sofa in the apartment's living area. "They've taken him from me."

"What? Taken who?" Javier squirmed in his seat. "Kione?"

She nodded.

"Sorry, Susan, I've been so snowed under with setting up the trans-space project." He frowned. "Who's taken him?"

"I'm not sure."

"What do you mean you're not sure?"

"When I arrived at TIAS and went down to the Green Level, he was gone. My team was packing up. They've shut down the project."

"We'd discussed this on the way back to Earth. There was the chance he'd be let out into the public—"

"No, Javier!" She held on to the arms of her chair with a vice-like grip. "They haven't released him. They gave him to someone else."

Javier wondered how much more stress she could be put through. "Have you talked to Minister Takashi?"

"He's not taking my calls. And the executive at the Institute won't tell me anything. Just that my services are no longer required. That asshole, Remy..."

Javier leaned over and placed a consoling hand on hers.

"With Nicolas halfway across the galaxy, and this"—she gestured down at her legs—"I don't know what to do. I'm scared for Kione."

"Don't worry, Susan, I'll get to the bottom of this." He smiled to reassure her, but inside was unsure where he'd begin.

TWENTY-THREE

Sierra Nevada Mountains, Earth

Jason thought nothing would compare to the wonders of the universe beyond his ancestral home. But when he visited Earth as a young boy, he made some concessions. There was, in fact, beauty on the third planet from the sun. And its memories had stayed with him his whole life.

All these years later, the Sierra Nevada Mountains were just as striking. In hindsight, after being booted from the service, he wondered if he should have gone there instead and lived off the land like the people of yore.

A snake probably would've eaten me.

He finished pitching his tent for the night and lit a fire. The sun dropped majestically beyond the horizon and he unfolded a chair, removing a bottle of Blue Jacket bourbon from his bag. Just as he was about to open it, his ears pricked up with an approaching sound.

He narrowed his eyes at headlights in the distance heading his way. He wondered what a hovercar could be doing so far from civilization. It climbed the hill and parked beside his own hovercar next to the tent. The driver's-side door opened, and Marissa Caldwell stepped out.

"How in the hell did you find me?" Jason asked.

She leaned on the hood of her car. "Oh, I've got my sources."

"But I didn't tell anyone I was coming here." Jason lugged a chair from the tray of his car and placed it beside his own.

Marissa walked over and sat. "Call it an educated guess then. When I couldn't find you and no one knew where you were, I assumed this was the place you'd be."

"I'm not sure how I feel about being so predictable."

"Well, you brought me here on more than a few occasions. I'll never forget the first time. We pitched our tent a little farther up the ridge and—"

"Yes, I remember." That night with Marissa had been the start of their turbulent relationship. A bond full of wonder and occasionally pure hell.

"It was fun." She smiled.

"Yes, it was."

"I even noticed the house on the way up here you told me was your great-great-great-grandfather's. It's still in one piece."

"Looks a little worse for wear. No idea who owns it now. It's still abandoned." Jason screwed the cap off his bourbon and took a swig. He passed it to Marissa.

"You don't have a nice chardonnay, do you?"

"Chardonnay? Ooh la-la," he teased.

"Give me the bottle." She laughed and snatched it from him, guzzling twice as much as him. She then winked and handed the bottle back.

"I misjudged you. You've still got it." From beneath his chair, he revealed a can of beans. "Something to eat?"

Marissa recoiled in horror, but it didn't stop Jason pulling the ring and pouring the beans into a pot over the fire.

"What brings you all the way up here anyway?" he asked.

"You know..."

He widened his eyes.

"The interview."

"Oh..." He blushed, doing his best not to sound disappointed. "I kind of came up here to be alone. I don't think—"

"So, I go to all this trouble, and you tell me to turn around?"

He stirred the pot figuratively and literally. "Well, not until after the beans...and more drink."

"I need to go back to Mars with something or my editor will be pissed."

"We can't have that, can we?" Jason drank some bourbon then tasted the beans. "I'm sure Malcolm's missing you, too."

"Marcus." Marissa took the bottle from him and laughed. "You did that deliberately."

"What?"

"You know his name is Marcus. My God, you're such an ass."

She was right. He wondered if he was actually jealous.

"You must admit, it's pretty funny," Jason said. "Marissa and Marcus. You almost have the same names. You don't have matching towels with your initials embroidered on them, do you?"

She sniggered, nearly spitting out her bourbon. "We do."

"Unbelievable."

She passed the bottle back, and Jason poured it into the beans for flavor. "I guess all you need is that white picket fence and you're set. Do the zoning authorities let you do that on Mars?"

Her laughter faded, and she seemed to stare out into nothingness.

"Marissa?"

She snapped out of it. "Sorry just...never mind."

Jason offered her the bourbon, which she downed a little too heartily. He finished cooking the beans and dispensed them in two separate bowls, giving her one and taking the other for himself. He couldn't help but notice the mood had changed. "Are you sure there's nothing you want to talk about?"

Marissa gazed into the fire. "Let's start with how you'd found out about the Iota particle readings at Frontier's Reach."

She took out a data tablet and a small recording device. For the rest of the night, Jason gave her the tell-all interview he'd promised her. They finished their beans and the bottle of bourbon, and Jason invited her inside his tent and asked her to stay.

He didn't expect her to take him up on his offer. But she did.

It was just like their first date all over again.

Tokyo Institute of Advanced Sciences - Tokyo, Earth

"What you're seeing here is the replication of Iota particles."

Minister Takashi watched through a microscope. To someone of his knowledge it would've looked like little more than small circles multiplying one after another. But it was significant.

"I didn't expect these results so quickly, Professor," he said to Javier.

When Javier witnessed it for the first time, he was equally amazed. "Professor Rahul has taken what I've discovered and methods he's been working with on various other programs. But I must stress this is but the first step of many. We still need to test the viability of the replicated particles."

"Meaning?"

"Meaning we have to be sure it has the same properties as the original. It's kind of like a clone. If one's copied over and over, they're no longer viable. We need to make sure that doesn't happen here."

"And how long will that take?"

For someone so impressed, he sounded mightily impatient, Javier lamented. "We have to establish their stability first. If they remain stable, we'll hopefully know in the next couple of days."

"Excellent. The president will be pleased."

Javier gestured toward the exit and they passed by other members of the project standing around workstations, inspecting blueprints and testing out various experiments.

"How are your other teams progressing?" Takashi asked him.

"We've had little success with Medical."

"Oh?"

"It was the one area my expertise was lacking. The team in charge don't have a lot to work with."

"I'm sure you'll steer them in the right direction," he said, as if it were so easy. "What about Delivery Systems?"

"That's what I wanted to discuss with you." Javier led the minister to the catwalk overlooking the several levels of the Institute's building. On the far wall staring back at them was a massive mural of the Saturn V rocket.

Javier peered around ensuring no one else was around. "I've been led to believe Kione is no longer at TIAS."

Takashi sighed. "You've been talking with Doctor Tai."

Javier nodded.

"What has this got to do with Delivery Systems?"

"I'll get to that." Javier leaned on the railing. "Where's Kione?"

"I can't tell you."

"Yet you can take Doctor Tai's work off her with the snap of your fingers after everything she's been through? She's the best in her field, and you know it."

"It wasn't my decision to make."

"You're the minister of defense, goddamn it!"

Takashi crossed his arms. "I don't like your tone, Professor."

Javier put a hand up in surrender. He remembered the proverb about honey and vinegar. "I apologize, Minister. But to shut down an entire program and—"

"The president felt, considering the situation we find ourselves in, that a new team should be placed in charge."

"At another facility?"

Takashi nodded. "There's still a lot we don't understand about his species. His contact with the sphere and the abilities he gained from it now make it more important than ever that we gain more knowledge about him."

"Respectfully, I think taking Doctor Tai off the project will only hold it back."

Takashi seemed in two minds about it. "Delivery Systems, Professor."

"Hmm? Oh. Yes, I'm happy to report we discovered a way of testing an Iota bombardment with the hope of creating a vortex. At least a small one. Once our particles are viable, that is."

Takashi tapped the railing with his wedding ring and smiled. "That's wonderful news."

"I will require something from you, however."

"Of course. Anything."

Javier put on his game face. "For starters, you need to tell me where Kione is."

Takashi frowned. "Professor—"

"This project has to succeed. Without me, it'll take much longer."

"You'd pull out of your own work? I think you're bluffing."

Javier peered out at the mural of the Saturn V. "I'm the Wernher von Braun of my day, Minister. Try me."

TWENTY-FOUR

Sierra Nevada Mountains, Earth

Jason put his arm over the other side of the camping bed, but his grasp found only emptiness. He opened his eyes to find the sun had risen, bathing the tent in a soft morning light.

Marissa?

He pulled himself up and crawled toward the end of the canvas where he unzipped the flap and poked his head out. Her car was gone, too. He walked outside toward the now burned-out fire where beside it lay an empty bourbon bottle.

Though he'd drank a sizeable portion of it, he'd recovered better than he had in a long time. He didn't need a degree to figure out why. Even years after their relationship had ended, the previous night together seemed like they'd never been apart. If anything, it was more passionate than any time before.

And while he felt fine, he could only imagine what

was going through Marissa's mind. She had her lover back home on Mars.

That's probably why she hightailed it out of here.

The sun beat down on him with purpose, and he wiped his forehead of sweat. He went back to his tent to find his wayward shirt, upturning the camping bed and finding it hiding in the corner. There was something else under it. He picked up the small device and pressed in the button on its side.

"Tell me about the natives of Psi-Aion. They're one of the neglected stories in all of this."

Jason switched off Marissa's recorder, which no doubt had his entire interview on. He quickly tidied the campsite and climbed into his hovercar, driving into the distance. By the time he reached Bakersfield Spaceport, the small terminal was a bustling hive of activity. Jason parked in the visiting lot and ran into the building. He peered up at the monitors and noted all the flights heading up to the various orbiting stations.

Not being able to make heads or tails of it all, he approached the customer service counter. The holographic representative smiled at him in an old-time blue hostess uniform which harked back to the twentieth century.

"Hello, sir. How can I help you today?"

"Which of the next services connect with transports to Mars?" he asked.

"There's the eight-fifteen to the Red Star. Unfortunately, there aren't any more seats—"

"I don't care about that. What gate's it leaving from?"

"Gate Twelve."

Jason glanced at his commband. He had six minutes. He checked the signage for directions and sprinted through the heart of the terminal.

Out of breath with a minute to spare, he approached the Red Star's staff at the airlock. "Has Marissa Caldwell boarded this transport?"

"Sir, we can't give out personal—"

He flashed his CDF identification badge from his pocket. "Official business."

They checked the ID and nodded. "She's aboard."

"What seat?"

One of them glanced at their data tablet. "Fourteen-B. But you can't go onboard, it's about to depart."

Jason ignored them and whizzed past, entering through the side airlock and passing by more bewildered staff. He studied the seat numbers above the windows until he found Marissa staring down at an electronic breakfast menu.

"Jason!" she almost squealed.

"You forgot something." He handed her the recorder.

Everyone looked in their direction, while a small contingent of the flight crew approached them.

"Oh?" She clutched at her handbag in the compartment beneath her seat and placed it inside. "Thank you, but you didn't have to come all this way. You could have sent the file instead."

He knew that, but in his heart of hearts, he wanted to see her again, just one more time.

The tallest of the flight attendants tapped him on the arm. "Sir, you need to leave the transport. We're about to launch."

Jason waved her away. "I get you needed to go, but to not even wake me and say goodbye."

Marissa's face reddened. "This is hardly the—"

"Sir!" the attendant said more forcefully.

"Yeah, just give me another minute."

She stormed off in a huff while her colleagues stood by the airlock.

"I know you want to forget last night happened, but it doesn't work that way." He got down on one knee, and everyone in the surrounding seats gasped in excitement.

"He's not proposing to me!" Marissa said to them. She then stared at Jason. "You're not, are you?

"No." Jason rolled his eyes. "Look, I'm sorry, I know I shouldn't have come, but with you heading home to your white picket fence, and me rejoining the service... Well, this time it might finally be it."

Though she was blushing with embarrassment, she smiled at Jason and put her hand on his.

Another hand found Jason as well. It dug into his shoulder like a bird of prey about to feast on its victim. He looked up at the transport's tall broad-shouldered pilot staring down on him.

"Badge or no badge, if you don't get off my ship, you and I are going to have problems," the pilot said.

Jason winked at Marissa and disembarked from the

craft under his own volition. He stood by the window inside the terminal and watched the orbital vehicle launch and disappear into the empty sky.

Feeling just as empty, he returned to his campsite alone.

Ganymede Station

The journey from Earth went so smoothly Aly found herself slightly bored. It wasn't that she wanted to repeat the drama of the last year, but there was something odd when there was so little crisis on the *Argo*. As captain and owner of the ship, they should have been the times to celebrate, but Aly couldn't help but struggle.

"Are you okay?"

She gazed beyond the fluffy pink beverage in front of her to her father's loving but concerned eyes. "I dunno, I guess I'm just thinking too much."

"Who taught you to do that?"

Aly laughed. "Whoever did, I should have a word with them."

"You're thinking about Jason, aren't you?"

She peered around the tavern they'd stumbled into. In the center was a circular bar. On one side were tables and chairs where patrons sat having quiet conversations between themselves, while on the other was a hypnotic cacophony of color and noise on a dance floor full of young people, who all seemed to have no cares in the world.

"Yeah, and Tyler." Aly frowned. "Things have changed so much."

Her father sipped at his beer. "I guess it doesn't make it easy sharing a ship with a pair of old codgers either."

He must've caught her looking across at the youngsters. "That's not it at all," she said.

"Alyssa, I get it. I was young once, too. It might have been during the Jurassic period, but I still remember." He glanced over his shoulder at the youthful revelers. "Why don't you go over there?"

"Because even I'm too old for that crowd."

"Ridiculous."

"I'm not a little girl anymore."

"You'll always be my little girl."

"That may be so, but unlike these kids, I've got a lot of responsibilities now." She stood. "Which includes checking over the engines before we return to Earth."

"If you won't go over there," he said, "perhaps I should."

Aly giggled and kissed him on the head. "Be home before midnight, and don't do anything I wouldn't do." She passed by the dancers and exited, making her way to Ganymede Station's hangar deck. Just as she'd left her, the *Argo* sat snuggly between a pair of small ore haulers.

Aly pressed on her commband, and the rear entry ramp extended. She climbed up it and activated the cargo bay's internal lighting with a mash of the panel beside the door. The hollow expanse would be once again full the next day with modules of lab samples for their return to Earth.

She took the elevator to A Deck and entered the engine room. It was messier than usual with all the other duties she had to perform. Something she'd have to rectify.

While she cleaned up the heap of tools on the maintenance console, her ears pricked up to a distant clatter. She stepped toward the hatchway and peered down the corridor.

But there was nothing there.

Then the rattle sounded again.

"Althaus?" she called out, knowing very well he wasn't one to be a prankster, especially in the mood he'd been in since leaving Earth. Not to mention the fact he said he was going to the station for some alone time.

Whatever that means.

She didn't want to know.

"Dad? I swear if you're trying to play games with me, I'll make you walk the plank." Aly slowly treaded down the corridor and stopped at a shuffling noise nearby, coming from the infirmary. She strolled in and pressed the light on beside the door.

She stared through the observation screen, but found nothing but emptiness.

She crept farther inside and searched around. It was clean. Much cleaner than her engine room.

However, something caught her eye. One of the medicine cabinets had been opened, and the stock had been ransacked. And lying on the floor beneath it sat a small handheld medical scanner.

She bent down and picked it up. "This isn't Dad's."

"That's right, it's mine."

Aly turned to find a tall, blond-haired man standing before her.

"Who the hell are you?" she gasped.

He didn't answer. Instead, he charged at her and knocked her to the deck. Her head slammed hard against the bulkhead, and her vision blurred and darkened. The last thing she remembered was the strange man hovering over her.

TWENTY-FIVE

Cargo Ship Argo

Kevin ran his hands over the bulkhead of the infirmary and waved his medical scanner through the air. He knelt and found one spot in particular that piqued his curiosity.

"This better be good, Rycroft."

Kevin craned his neck at Althaus who walked through the hatchway. "Don't worry, there'll be plenty more opportunities between now and the end of our contract to visit Ganymede's ladies of the night."

Althaus crossed his arms, clearly not too impressed by the comment. "What are you doing down there?"

"Alyssa's missing."

"What!" Althaus ambled over to him and helped him up. "Did she say if she was going anywhere?"

"Only back to the *Argo*."

"Have you tried reaching her on her commband?"

"She's not responding." Kevin showed Althaus the

readings on his scanner. "Seems she did return. Someone attempted to clean it up, but they must've been in a hurry. Blood and skin. Both hers, and both fresh within the last hour." He walked over to the medical console and logged on to the ship's main computer. "And from what I can tell, all the logs have been wiped. No one in or out of the ship since the three of us left earlier in the evening."

Althaus brushed past him and stabbed at the controls, shaking his head. "Whoever did this knew what they were doing."

"What would someone want with her?" All of Kevin's worst nightmares flashed before him. He could only hope she was still alive and the speck of blood he'd found wasn't part of a larger spill.

"I'm not sure," Althaus pondered, "but we better go to the station's security office."

Tokyo Institute of Advanced Sciences - Tokyo, Earth

Susan entered the large communal dining area of the Institute, passing by the odd strange look, and a few warm smiles. On the other side of the hall, Javier stood and walked toward her.

"Thank you for coming, Susan. I've got us a table." He gestured to one of the secluded sections and took a seat.

Susan directed her chair to sit opposite him.

"I would've come to see you but—"

"You don't need to apologize, Javier," she assured

him. "I understand how much stress this project's putting you under."

"I did some digging." He lowered his voice. "Well, I guess that's not quite true. I went straight to Takashi."

She raised her brow. "What did he say?"

Javier checked around to make sure no one was eavesdropping. "Kione's in a facility in Edinburgh."

"Scotland?"

He nodded.

"What are they doing to him?"

"Takashi was very cagey about much of the specifics, but I got you a meeting with the head of the program." He placed a data tablet between them with a Pan-Atlantic ticket on it. "I've booked you on a transport there this evening."

Susan smiled. "You really are a good friend."

"I feel guilty not coming with you. I'm due to take a flight of my own to Luna. If I'd known—"

"Javier, you've done more than I thought you could."

He reached over and held her hand. "Do what you need, to get to the bottom of this, okay?"

Count on it.

Texas, Earth

The countryside was flat. Really flat.

When Jason left the spaceport and picked up his rental hovercar, he pointed it down one of the two roads out of town and followed the signs all the way toward his destination.

He hit a slight incline and barreled up a long track until he reached a solitary property out in the middle of nowhere. At the gate, a wooden sign greeted him: WELCOME TO SHILA RANCH.

He drove past it and pulled up at a large but quaint ranch house surrounded by old-style fences. If Jason didn't know any better, he'd swear he'd traveled back in time to the Wild West of the late eighteen-hundreds. He got out of the rental and knocked on the front door. But no one answered. He peered through the window and around the property. There wasn't a soul in sight. Returning to his car, he wondered if he'd got his dates mixed up.

Then, in the hovercar window's reflection, he spotted movement. On the other side of the ranch, a horse raced across the field. Someone was riding it and seemed to be pretty good at it, too.

He strode over to the wooden fence to admire the magnificent beast in action. Jason had never ridden a horse. They weren't common on a cargo ship and kind of frightened him. Ships did what they were told. A horse, however...they had a mind of their own.

The rider changed direction and headed toward him at a slow gallop. The closer they got to him, the clearer the person on the back of the horse became.

She removed her sunglasses and threw him her riding helmet, which he caught.

He put his hand up to guard his eyes from the sun. "Captain Shila."

"Commander Cassidy." She stepped down from the horse and grabbed the reins. "I assume you found the place all right?"

He nodded. "It's nice country out here."

"Nicer than Sierra Nevada?"

Jason was impressed. She'd obviously done her homework. "Both have their pros and cons."

"I hope you don't sit on the fence too often. I'm after decisiveness in my executive officer."

Jason chuckled. "I think if you've read my file, you'll find that's not a quality I lack."

Shila eyed him as if trying to sum him up. She put her sunglasses back on and made her way toward the ranch house with Jason trailing not far behind.

"I have to admit, when I checked your personnel file, I wondered why the hell I was getting shafted with you. You were discharged from the service for striking a superior officer, being a drunkard, and flying a fighter into an asteroid field without permission. But I understand how the system works. With the war over, we saw a major drop in recruits. What better way to get those numbers up than by bringing the hero of Orion V back into the fold?"

Jason knew she was right but hadn't heard someone say it so succinctly. It wasn't a pleasant thing to be told.

"With that said, when I delved further, I discovered the Jason Cassidy who fought during the war. The one with all the medals. The one who was a hell of a pilot."

Shila strolled into the stable, and Jason ducked under the fence to follow her in. She placed the horse in a box stall and settled him inside.

"My question to you is, are you going to be the Jason Cassidy who fought during the war or the drunk who made a fool of himself afterwards?"

"I assure you, I'm not here to make up the numbers," Jason said.

"Good." She closed the door of the box stall and stood directly in front of him. "Because if you ever try to pull the same crap you did on Captain Kaufman, I'll knock you so hard on your ass your head will spin. Do I make myself clear?"

"Crystal."

She put out her hand and smiled. "Welcome to the team."

TWENTY-SIX

Ganymede Station

The night turned the small metropolis of Ganymede Station into a much seedier proposition than earlier in the evening. Kevin thought back to the kids he'd seen having fun in the bar. They'd probably moved on and were now looking for more action while continuing to get heavily liquored up.

At the heart of the station, he and Althaus found the administration hub. All the offices were empty apart from one. Kevin knocked on the door. With no reply, he spotted a small terminal and pressed it in. When he didn't get a reply again, he slammed the panel with his fist.

"Goddamn it, open up!"

"What is it?" asked the voice through the intercom, a little too lackadaisical for his liking.

"We want to check your cameras and report a

missing individual," Kevin told him in the calmest manner he could muster.

An audible sigh sounded from the other end, and the door clicked open. Kevin and Althaus walked in and followed the lights up a flight of stairs.

The night shift security officer sat behind a transparent screen at a desk with several monitors surrounding him—all with video feeds from around the station. The man darted his eyes from one to the other while his arm was firmly entrenched elbow deep in a bag of potato chips.

Kevin squinted at the name badge affixed to the shirt many sizes too small for him. "Bill, we need footage from the hangar deck between eighteen hundred and twenty-one hundred tonight. Specifically, any camera pointing at the *Cargo Ship Argo*."

Bill was slow to the punch but eventually pushed his chips aside and prodded at his console. The largest of the monitors behind him changed to an image of the *Argo*'s stern with a time index of eighteen-oh-four.

Althaus was the first to emerge from the ship's downed ramp, followed by Kevin and Alyssa.

"Okay, that's when we all left the *Argo* for the night," Kevin observed.

Alyssa closed the ramp with her commband, sealing the ship shut. They watched the footage play at an accelerated speed all the way through to the moment Kevin returned to the *Argo* after finishing up at the bar. The time index was twenty fifty-three.

"Wait. Stop," Kevin said.

Bill froze the image.

"This doesn't make sense. Alyssa would have come back to the ship between the times of twenty-fifteen and twenty-thirty. I have proof of that from her blood in the infirmary."

"Are you sure you're not mistaken?" Bill asked.

Kevin slid a data tablet through the gap in the security screen, doing his best not to knock the packet of chips over. "I need you to put out an alert. This is the person who's missing."

Bill looked over the file and uploaded the relevant details into the system. Behind him, an image of Alyssa appeared with the word MISSING above her in bold red letters. He passed the tablet back to Kevin. "If we find out any information, we'll contact you."

Kevin hated how blasé the man was about it. He knew disappearances in places like Ganymede Station happened a lot, and the officer was probably immune to it all, but this was his daughter who was missing, and it was killing him inside.

Althaus put a hand on the security screen. "Can you replay the footage from time index twenty-ten to twenty twenty-five again?"

Bill stared at him. "And what's that going to achieve?"

"Please. It's important."

Kevin had never heard Althaus say please in his whole life. He was obviously onto something. Bill sighed and did as requested.

After the initial time index, the image blurred for a split second. "Stop," Althaus said. "What's that?"

Bill studied it closely. "Sometimes our security systems get affected by interference from Jupiter, depending on Ganymede's orbit. Seems like that could be it."

"Resume the footage."

The blur returned past the second time index, and Althaus instructed him to stop again. "The first part of the impaired vision is at twenty-fourteen and the second at twenty twenty-three. Somewhere in between that that is when Alyssa should've come back to the *Argo*."

"What are you suggesting?" Bill asked.

Yes, what are you suggesting?

Althaus glanced down into the palm of his hand and then over at Kevin. "We've taken enough of your time. Let's go, Rycroft."

Kevin followed him down the flight of stairs and out into the corridors of the empty administration hub. "What was that all about, Althaus?"

"If I were to place money on it, I'd say someone hacked into the security system to alter that footage."

"If that's the case, how do we find out who did it?"

Althaus pulled out a small electronic device from his palm. "While we were in there, I did a little hacking of my own. Let's see what I found."

Cargo Ship Argo

"Connection established."

Conrad peered down at the piece of hardware on the operations station to ensure what the computer had relayed was accurate.

Rycroft gripped the back of his chair tighter than Conrad was comfortable with. But he couldn't blame how his normally calm and collected comrade felt. It was the same reaction he'd had knowing Tyler was light-years away with no avenue home. And while he was still fuming about the kid giving the ship to Alyssa, he didn't want to lose her.

Conrad ran his hands over the console and brought up a register of every computer technician employed on Ganymede Station.

"You hacked into their entire computer network?" Rycroft said incredulously.

"More or less." There were one hundred and eighty-three staff in total. Conrad had to narrow it down, so he pressed in another key, and a list of bank records appeared next to each name.

"And you've got their bank details?"

Conrad glanced back at him. "Do you want your daughter back or not?"

"Of course. I'd just forgotten how good you are at this." Rycroft leaned in. "What are you thinking?"

"I figure the computer systems of Ganymede Station are relatively secure, no thanks to their lax security department. If they were tampered with, it'd be at the hands of a technician."

"And you think someone paid them to do it?"

"Who better than a poor-ass tech jockey." Conrad waited for the computer to complete the crosscheck with each name to find any financial irregularity. When the search was finished, one name popped up. He opened the file. "Wyatt Rapier. For the past week, he received between two hundred and four hundred credits daily into his three different accounts."

"Where's the money coming from?" Rycroft asked.

"Several personal accounts. Unless he's a gigolo, I'd say they're dummies. They're doing it this way so the schmuck doesn't get flagged. Lucky for us, my software has more stringent algorithms."

"Do you have an address for this Wyatt Rapier?"

Conrad brought up the data and nodded. "Apartment two-forty-three, block D of the habitat section."

Rycroft bolted for the exit. "Time to pay Mister Rapier a visit."

Ganymede Station

Wyatt Rapier's neighborhood was a rough one. The corridors were filthy, the bulkheads were lined with graffiti, and vagrants stumbled throughout, seeking their next hit. Kevin and Althaus rounded the corner and approached the door with the number two-forty-three on it.

Kevin pressed the door chime on the grimy panel,

but no one answered. He viewed the camera above and waved. "Hello."

"Who is it?" the voice replied on the other side of the intercom.

"We've come to ask you a few questions?"

"I'm busy right now."

"It's important. My daughter's missing and—"

"I'm sorry to hear that, but unless you're security, I'm not letting anyone in."

Kevin rolled his eyes and he looked over at Althaus who was standing on the opposite side of the door, appearing as devious as ever. "You have one last chance to open up, or we're coming in—"

"I'm not letting—"

"Time's up." Althaus ran his device over the door, and it slid open. He bounded into the room, catching Rapier off guard.

Kevin would usually be the peacemaker in such a situation, but Alyssa's life was on the line. If it weren't for Althaus, he'd be the one ramming Rapier's throat against the wall.

"Now listen here, kid, and listen good. You're going to answer our questions or there'll be hell to pay." Althaus gripped Rapier's neck as if he was about to squeeze the life out of him. "Why did you tamper with the security systems?"

"I'm not sure what—" the petrified man tried to spit out.

"You didn't understand me, did you? If you don't

tell me what we want to know, I'll drag you down to the lower level and space you out the nearest airlock."

Rapier struggled under the force.

"Let him go," Kevin said to him. "Just a little."

Althaus loosened his hold.

The young man took in a few deep breaths. "He told me if I ratted, he'd kill me."

"Who?" Kevin asked.

"He didn't tell me his name."

Althaus banged him against the bulkhead again.

Kevin put a hand on his shoulder, eyeing him to let the younger man speak. "Did he pay you to tamper with the security systems?"

Rapier nodded.

"Why?"

"I'm not sure. I can only guess he wanted to get on a ship for some reason."

Kevin paced in front of him. "And he said nothing about a kidnapping?"

"No. He gave me the date and times to alter the security footage so it appeared he hadn't been aboard."

"You'll be in a lot of trouble when the authorities find out about this," Althaus told him.

"Oh, please, I beg of you, don't tell—"

"They can't have been after Alyssa," Kevin pondered.

Althaus glanced back at him. "What?"

"Whoever went on the *Argo* was specific enough to do it when none of us were aboard. Did you put a booking in it at Madam Mao's?"

Althaus's face reddened.

"Did you?" Kevin asked again.

"Yes," he finally said.

"Aly and I booked a booth for dinner and drinks at the bar. He knew about those bookings and expected no one to be on the *Argo* at that time."

"But Alyssa went back early."

"Right. She probably caught him in the middle of whatever he was doing." Kevin pounded his fist against the wall. "She could very well be dead!"

Althaus pushed Rapier farther up the bulkhead, lifting his feet off the deck. "You don't know your client's name, but he must have approached you somehow to ask for your services."

"We met at a bar," he blurted out.

"Which bar?"

"The Ganymede Six."

"When?"

"A few nights ago. The nineteenth."

"What time?"

"I—"

Althaus squeezed harder. "What time did you meet him?"

"I think it was between twenty-one hundred and twenty-two hundred." Rapier's eyeballs were as wide as Jupiter's orbit.

"You think?"

"I know. I know," he groveled.

Althaus glared at him and plonked him back down. "Come on, Rycroft, let's get out of here."

The pair made their way to the door.

"Hey," Rapier called out.

They both turned to him while he adjusted his scuffed-up clothes. "I hope you find her."

Kevin wanted to punch the man's lights out. But that'd take too much precious time away from finding his daughter.

If she's still alive.

TWENTY-SEVEN

Cargo Ship Argo

The footage from the bar whizzed by at a sped-up rate. It was the fifth angle they'd checked from the evening of Rapier's meeting with his contact.

Kevin clenched his fists. "The longer this takes, the less—"

"Rycroft." Althaus glanced back at him from his seat at the operations console. "Calm down."

Kevin paced the bridge and returned as something caught his eye on the monitor. "Hold on. Do you see that? Near the wall?"

Althaus zoomed in on the frozen image at a pair of legs in the top right-hand corner. He played the footage, and the person entered the bar.

Kevin pointed to him. "That's Rapier."

"You're right, I'd recognize that lily-livered stride anywhere."

"He's heading to the booth. Can you get a camera

above him?"

Althaus ran his hands over the console and another view popped up from over the booth. He resumed the video, and they observed Rapier sitting down. Further into the feed, someone strode toward him and sat opposite. He was taller than Rapier and wore his long blond hair in a ponytail.

"This must be the guy. Can you get a tight shot in on his face?" Kevin asked.

"It's difficult because he's looking away from the camera." Althaus played through the vision until the blond man got up and walked off. He paused it, capturing one side of his face. "That's the best I can do. He bypasses every other camera in the place."

Kevin narrowed his eyes. "Will it be enough?"

"Maybe." Althaus zoomed in and extrapolated. The computer used the vision it had and filled in the blanks. A few moments later, a more complete picture emerged.

Kevin stared at the face. So much so, he thought he might burn a hole through the monitor. "I assume you hacked into the docking manifests?"

Althaus nodded and brought up the details of every single ship that had visited Ganymede Station within the last month. "It's a large list."

He plugged in a search algorithm, and the computer scrolled through all the data available.

A face finally appeared.

It was like the other. But this one was real. Kevin could look into this one's eyes.

What have you done with my little girl?

"His name is Darius Lok," Althaus read from the profile before him.

"Ship?"

"Owner and operator of *The Thor's Hammer*—a single-pilot craft."

"Location?"

Althaus brought up the data. "He left Ganymede Station at twenty-one hundred hours."

"Right after he finished whatever he did on the *Argo*." Kevin rubbed bridge of his nose. "Did he leave a flight plan?"

Althaus nodded. "Europa Station. But that doesn't mean—"

"I know. It might be a dummy flight plan to cover his tracks. Check the scanner logs. When he left the station, did his ship depart on a trajectory toward Europa?"

The data appeared on the monitor and they both peered at the small dot representing *The Thor's Hammer* moving from the station and following a line away from it toward Ganymede's sister moon.

Althaus shook his head. "This doesn't mean he didn't alter his course after leaving scanning range."

"Right, but we have to start somewhere." Kevin hurried over to the helm. "Get clearance from station control. I'll do the pre-flights."

The Thor's Hammer

Aly opened her eyes.

It was just as dark as it had been under her eyelids.

While her vision adjusted, she felt around her surroundings with her hands. There was a vibration beneath her feet.

I'm on a ship.

The room was empty. The floor was only three meters square, and the ceiling was only half a meter above her head. There were walls on three sides, and at the forth, a set of bars she could barely put her arms through.

What the hell happened?

She replayed everything in her mind since returning to the *Argo* after her evening with her father in the bar. She remembered arriving aboard, going to the engine room, and then...

I heard a noise in the infirmary.

A light blinked on outside her cell, and a man approached her. He was tall and dressed in dark clothes. He had long blond hair and a pair of deep-blue eyes.

The memory came back to her. "You struck me!"

She grabbed the bars of the cell with one hand and the back of her skull with the other. It was still tender from the hit she'd taken on the bulkhead.

"I patched the wound," he said to her. "It wasn't as bad as I'd thought."

"What were you doing aboard the *Argo*?" Aly demanded.

"You're welcome." From behind his back he pulled out a tray of food filled with meat and rice. He placed it through a small hatch in the bars and slid it across to her. She turned her nose up.

"You should eat," he told her.

Aly crossed her arms.

"Your loss." He turned away.

Aly clutched at the bars. "What do you want from me?"

His head swiveled around. "Nothing."

"Then why am I—?"

"I had valuable work I needed to do aboard your ship—"

"What did you do?" Aly's thoughts moved to her father, realizing he must be having a fit right now at her disappearance. Then she remembered something else. "You had a medical scanner in your hand. What were you after?"

The man regarded her as if she was too smart for her own good. "I'm never one to be as careless as I have been. I get paid a lot of money to keep things under wraps. You've gotten in the way of that."

Aly regretted opening her mouth. "I don't know what you were looking for, so there isn't much point keeping me here. If you let me go, I won't tell anyone what happened."

"My employers wouldn't like that. They're not fond of leaving witnesses around. And I enjoy being paid. So, you can see the bind I'm in."

She didn't like the sound of that. "What are you going to do with me?"

"Eat your food." He reentered the darkness, leaving her to ponder.

He'd at least had the courtesy to leave the light on,

but Aly wondered how long until he turned hers off for good. The hairs on the back of her neck stood on end. She glanced down at her tray and jabbed at it. It smelled horrendous.

Probably rat.

She pushed it aside.

Aly wondered if her dad would have any idea how to find her. For all she knew, he probably thought she was dead. Her chest heaved, and she wanted to vomit. But there was no time for that. It would be up to her to find a way out.

Aly could tell her cell was a makeshift one by the bar's installation in the bulkheads, which meant she may have a chance at escaping. She peered at the light just outside her confinement.

Lucky I have skinny arms.

TWENTY-EIGHT

Edinburgh, Earth

Susan had always wanted to visit Scotland. As a child, she'd dreamed of seeing the majestic castles and pretended she was a character in one of the many fantasy books she used to read. She probably would have enjoyed the scenic vistas more if it weren't for the reason she was there.

After a short hovercar ride from the spaceport to the outskirts of the city, she arrived at the building where Kione was being held. The dark-gray, three-story structure sat on the misty backdrop of rolling green hills. In the distance, there was even one of those castles she'd envisioned.

Down the steep road, the driver took her through the main checkpoint to check her security credentials, and then onto the entrance of the building. With the help of a specialized ramp, she rolled her chair from the car toward the facility.

Susan waited and waited, glancing at the driver whose face was like a stone, belaying any emotion. Then the entrance opened.

A young woman stepped out and walked toward her. "Doctor Tai. Please come this way." She ushered her through into a cold and dank lobby. Apart from a few guards, there wasn't a soul anywhere.

Susan followed the woman to an elevator and entered. Up three levels, she accompanied her escort into more empty corridors. Her designated greeter then led her into a room overlooking the hills.

"The doctor will be with you shortly." With that, she turned on her heels and scurried out.

Susan moved toward the window where the fog was lifting, getting a much better view of the ancient castle. She smiled, imagining herself in some juvenile fairy tale in the highest tower waiting for her prince charming. Then her smile faded. She had to remind herself she was no castle princess trapped in her chair and her prince charming was stuck somewhere hundreds of light-years away.

"It's beautiful, isn't it?"

In the glass's reflection, a figure stood at the door behind her. She brought her chair around, and the dark-haired man smiled.

"You should be so lucky. While TIAS is wonderful, it doesn't have the serenity you have here." Susan raised an eyebrow. "Though it's almost too serene. There are so few people in your facility."

"They told me you were inquisitive." The man stepped toward her.

"Do you blame me?"

"No, not at all." He gestured toward a table at the center of the room.

She approached it, and he took the seat on the opposite side.

"My name's Doctor Charles Whitlowe. My facility, unlike TIAS, relies on a much smaller staff. We're set up simply for the continued study of Kione, and I only brought in the people I most trust."

"Fair enough."

"I apologize. I realize how this probably makes you feel. But when the Ministry approached me for the opportunity, I couldn't say no."

"I would've done the same."

"But it doesn't make it anymore right..."

"I won't lie, when I was replaced, it felt like all my work had been in vain."

"I'm sure the Ministry of Defense don't think any less of your studies. The data you and your predecessors compiled on Kione is extensive. I believe they just wanted a second opinion. Especially considering the new abilities he's displayed."

"They asked you to exploit those abilities, didn't they?"

Whitlowe put his hands up in surrender. "I won't lie, they're naturally curious."

"Naturally." Susan frowned. "What kind of background do you have, Doctor? I've never heard of you or seen you at any medical conferences."

He chuckled. "I guess we mingle in different circles. Would you like to observe my methods? You obviously care greatly for Kione. Let me put your mind at ease with what I do here."

He hadn't answered her question, but she very much wanted an opportunity to snoop. "Lead the way."

For the next hour, Doctor Whitlowe showed her through all the labs, let her check over all the equipment, and allowed her to talk to his assisting staff. What she found was a similar operation to the one she had at the Institute, with some minor differences. What she didn't see was the silver bullet that would unravel Kione's secrets, but she couldn't fault Whitlowe's confidence.

When they exited the lab, Whitlowe stopped outside in the corridor and turned to her. "What did you think?"

"You've put a lot of work into setting up this program." Susan humored him. In reality, he was out of his depth. But she wasn't about to insult the man. He was very accommodating with everything he'd shown her.

"I'm glad you approve."

"There is one more thing..."

Whitlowe raised an eyebrow.

"I'd like to see Kione."

He smiled and led her through to another room. It was set out similarly to the room upstairs, but there were no windows. A pale light filtered down from the ceiling, along with several cameras pointing in several directions.

"Wait here, Doctor," Whitlowe instructed her.

He left her by herself, and she moved near one of the tables.

After a few moments, another door opened, and Kione stepped out, smiling. "Doctor, it's good to see you." He sat opposite her with wide open eyes. "I didn't know whether I'd get another chance after being transferred from TIAS."

"Professor Petit pulled a few strings," she said, studying his features closely. "How are you? How are they treating you?"

"While it's a lot different to the Institute, Doctor Whitlowe and his team have made me most welcome."

"What about the testing? Have they—?"

"You don't have to fear, Doctor." He shook his head. "I was anxious at first but I quickly discovered I was worrying over nothing."

She stared at him, unable to look away from the same smile he had when he walked in. "As long as you're happy here, I guess I can't really complain."

"Trust me, Doctor, I am." He stood from his chair. "While I've enjoyed the visit, you must understand I have much to do." He stepped toward her and bent down, putting a hand on hers.

An image flashed in Susan's mind.

It was Kione.

He lay on a bed with several intravenous drips connected to his arms. His body convulsed against his restraints.

And his scream jangled her bones.

Susan flashed back to reality with Kione staring down at her, grinning.

What have I just experienced?

Jason Cassidy had told her of what he'd encountered with Kione on the Seeker ship. All the things he'd done with his mind. But the sphere was gone, he shouldn't have had those abilities.

How did you do that?

She glanced up at the cameras.

And what are they doing to you here?

Kione walked back through the door and disappeared from her life once again.

TWENTY-NINE

Serenity Science Station - Luna

Javier stared from the viewport, enchanted by the beauty of the barren yet still mysterious moon, while his transport pod dived for the surface. Beyond it, lay the land-based scientific facility he'd once called home, and while he much preferred Tokyo, he was fond of his time on Luna, especially getting to marvel at the magnificent sunrises.

The pod arrived on the smaller of the two landing pads, and after the pressurization of the hangar deck, the pilot gave Javier the go-head to disembark. He unbuckled his belt and walked through the airlock and down the extended ramp. Waiting for him at the bottom appeared a familiar face. He couldn't believe he hadn't seen her for over eighteen months. He lamented that it hadn't been long enough.

"Hello, Javier," she greeted him frostily.

Javier put out a hand to Professor Song Ji-min, and

she begrudgingly shook it. "It's nice to see you, Song. I'm sorry it isn't under better circumstances."

She glared at him. "The projects of the famous Javier Petit always take precedence over everyone else's, don't they?"

"You know I wouldn't be here unless I really needed to. The Ministry of Defense has me over a barrel with this trans-space project. They want results."

"You could've asked me. You didn't have to go over my head."

He chuckled. "Would you have said yes?"

She frowned and ushered him toward the door. Javier followed her out into the corridor of the old base where the quaint surroundings hadn't changed.

He couldn't help but notice the anger bubbling beneath Song's calm demeanor. The pair were two of the most accomplished scientists of their age. Over their careers, they'd become rivals, always fighting over what funding came their way. After the Earth-Centauri War, the Ministry of Defense had come to the Institute looking for one of them to head the new Vladivostok Project to create a fail-safe, energy-based planetary defense system. The conflict was still in people's minds, and President Jarret wanted Earth protected at all costs if further hostilities broke out. Both Javier and Song sought to be the lead scientist, but he'd won out, giving the Ministry the best presentation to accomplish their goal.

However, because Song's expertise impressed them so much, they placed her as his second-in-charge of the program. To say they butted heads would be an understatement. When Minister Takashi came calling after the discovery of the sphere on Orion V, they'd transferred Javier out and put Song in his place.

"When I got back to Earth, I read up on your progress with the Vladivostok Project. You've done a lot of great work here," he said to her, doing his best to soothe any wounds.

"Not as much as I'd hoped." Her glare softened. "The Ministry's getting impatient."

"They've been leaning on you?"

"They told me if they don't see any significant results soon, they'll pull me from the project." She chuckled dryly. "And here you are, the lead on a new program, already talking about tests, while hijacking my work to see them through."

And we were doing so well.

"To be fair, I've been working on the trans-space program for the past six months on my voyage home. As far as commandeering your work, I'm simply borrowing Nora. Once I've done my tests, I'll—"

"Be gone. Really?" Song shook her head. "I've been reading up on your work, too. If you have even the faintest success creating a trans-space corridor with Nora, the Ministry of Defense will come in here, rip up my program's mandate, and throw me out the door."

Javier didn't know what to say. He knew how things worked, and she was right.

They walked through a large set of doors and into the vast main laboratory. In the heart of the circular room, behind a transparent screen sat Nora—The prototype of the Vladivostok Project. She was a cylindrical-shaped object with rounded edges and a conical emitter on one end. Its purpose was to be a fully fledged automated defense weapon. One of many. So far, it hadn't lived up to expectations. Javier hoped if it didn't see the light of day in its original capacity it could at least be of some help to him.

UECS Sabre

Jason tried to remember the last time he'd been on a CDF ship. It would've been when he'd left the Olbers Training Station after his dishonorable discharge. It seemed like a lifetime ago. As he walked through the airlock of the *Sabre*, the hairs on the back of his neck stood on end. It was as if the ghost of Christian Nash marched alongside him. Jason liked to think his old friend would be happy for him.

Watching everyone go past in their uniforms made him feel like a pariah. More so than he did already. He wondered what it woud be like when he was back in one of those uniforms.

"Commander Cassidy?"

He turned to a young officer behind him. "Yes," he said to her.

"I'm Ensign Jefferson, sir. I've been instructed to take you to Captain Shila," she gestured down the corridor with a blank expression. "Would you come this way?"

"Of course." He followed her through the long halls of the ship, which dwarfed the *Argo's* tiny interior. And because of the refit, the *Sabre* appeared so new. From the computer panels to the freshly painted bulkheads. There wasn't a scratch anywhere. But there was something about it...

There's no soul here.

He wondered if he was finding a newfound appreciation for the *Argo*. After spending so much of his adolescent life wanting to flee the quaint cargo ship, he'd begun seeing it in a new light. Especially with everything they'd gone through aboard her.

What's wrong with me?

Ahead of him a familiar face appeared. Not to mention the familiar strut to go with it. "Rao!"

He'd read up on the ship's personnel files and knew he'd bump into his old shipmate at some point. He was new to the ship as well, taking the chief engineer's post.

Lieutenant Commander Rao handed a subordinate a data tablet and approached Jason. "Commander Cassidy."

He shook his hand and smiled. But the grin on Rao's face revealed an awkwardness Jason had never seen before.

"How long has it been?" he asked.

"Since the *Raptor*," Rao replied.

"Oh."

An uncomfortable silence permeated between them, and Jefferson cleared her throat to get his attention.

"Well," Jason said. "It's good to see you again. We must start a poker game some time."

"Sure." Rao nodded uncommittedly. "If you'll excuse me, sir."

"I'll catch you later."

The *Sabre's* new chief engineer hurried off down the corridor, and Jason frowned. Jefferson gestured in the opposite direction, and he entered the elevator behind her.

The doors swished open at their destination, and they both walked out through a hatchway onto the *Sabre's* command deck. Like the rest of the ship, it was new and bright. For an instant he became the center of attention. Most hid their thoughts, but others let their faces betray their feelings toward him. Whether it was because of his discharge from the service or how he'd come in and leapfrogged many other able officers in rank, he was obviously not welcome. He had a lot of work to do to gain their trust.

"Commander Cassidy." Captain Shila stood at the central command station, waving him toward her.

He walked down the steps into the pit. "Commander Cassidy reporting for duty, Captain."

She nodded. "Welcome aboard the *Sabre*. What do you think of her?"

Jason glanced around the bridge and looked down at his feet, remembering Captain Pizzeri and Commander Riggs dead in the same spot on the *Raptor*.

"It's a remarkable ship, Captain."

"I'm glad you approve." She turned to Jefferson.

"Have the quartermaster fetch the commander his uniform."

"It's taken care of, Captain. They're already in the commander's quarters."

"Excellent." She nodded. "Get yourself suited up."

"Aye," Jason said.

Ensign Jefferson led him from the command deck and up another two decks where she showed him to his quarters. When he entered, he thought he'd arrived at a luxury hotel. The room was three times the size of his cabin on the *Argo*. It had its own bathroom and kitchen amenities along with everything else he could have wanted. However, it wasn't quite the same without the posters of Annabelle Pearl or Sky Jensen peering down at him from the wall.

He put his bags on the bed and opened the closet. Inside he found a full line of blue CDF uniforms for every day of the week. He took one off its coat hanger and stared at it, touching the gold commander rank pins on the collar.

The more things change, the more things stay the same...

THIRTY

Cargo Ship Argo

Kevin hadn't bitten his nails for years. It'd been a habit he'd long since kicked. In the last few hours, however, he'd taken up the old practice and eaten them down to their nubs.

Sitting at the helm the whole time staring at Jupiter hadn't helped matters. It was frustrating traveling in the Jovian system of moons, because from their perspective, the gas giant's vast size made it seem like they weren't moving, when in reality they were blasting along at breakneck speed.

"There it is," Althaus said from the operations station.

Kevin squinted at the icy surface of Europa appearing as a speck in the distance. As the *Argo* moved ever closer, the moon got larger and the distinct circular shape of its orbiting facility became more apparent.

"Open a commlink to Europa Station," Kevin told him.

Althaus did as instructed. "You're on."

"This is Kevin Rycroft of the *Cargo Ship Argo*."

"This is Europa Station. Go ahead," came the reply.

"I'm after information regarding the whereabouts of a ship. It's called *The Thor's Hammer*. We—"

"I'm sorry, Mister Rycroft, but all flight plans are strictly confidential."

"We've just come from Ganymede Station after reporting a missing person."

"Stand by."

Silence ensued. Too much of it for Kevin's liking.

"We've checked our computer banks. Is this in regard to Alyssa Rycroft?"

"That's right."

"There's nothing in this report suggesting The Thor's Hammer *is linked to her disappearance."*

"Uh, well..." Kevin glanced at Althaus. "We came to that determination ourselves. Look, this is my daughter. I'm not sure if she's dead or alive, but we know the operator of this ship has something to do with it. If you could find it in your heart—"

"Stand by." The silence followed again. *"That's a negative,* Argo. The Thor's Hammer *has not appeared on any of our scanners."*

Kevin dropped his head. "Thank you, Europa Station." While he was appreciative, they'd bent the rules to give him the information he was after, it left their search at a dead end.

The Thor's Hammer

"Come on, ignite!"

Aly put the two protruding wires together out of the light fitting from the ceiling and placed them on the locking mechanism of her cell. She stood back, and a small spark flew from the lock. She smiled and pushed her cage open with a forceful nudge.

The ship's engine hummed beneath her feet, and the sound changed ever so slightly. The ship was slowing down.

She walked from the darkness toward a glimmer of light peeking around the corner of a bulkhead. On the other side was a kitchenette and open-plan quarters with a bed to the side. On a desk near it were a pile of data tablets. She checked, making sure the coast was clear, and trawled through them. They were files on all different kinds of people. From upstanding citizens to criminals, from the rich to the poor. There were even children.

He's a bounty hunter.

By what she gathered going through all the paperwork he was an odd-job man hired to take out targets, kidnap for ransom, and any other unscrupulous work he could get his hands on. One data tablet caught her eye more than any other. On it was an image of Kione.

The feel of the deck plates beneath her altered, and she looked over at the ladder chute near the kitchen, leading up one level. She put the data tablet down and climbed the rungs, bobbing her head upward as inconspicuously as possible. At the bow of the deck was the cockpit, where her captor sat in a single chair, staring in the opposite direction through the forward viewport.

They approached another vessel, and they continued to slow.

"This is Darius Lok of *The Thor's Hammer* requesting landing," he said over a commlink.

"You're clear," came the reply over the speakers.

Lok toggled at the helm controls and steered the ship toward the hangar deck of the much larger ship ahead. Aly ducked her head to be certain she wasn't spotted.

Lok maneuvered through the hangar deck doors and down onto the landing area. He unbuckled himself from his harness and stood.

Aly quickly and quietly slid down the ladder chute and returned to her confinement. She pushed the loose wiring of the light back into its fitting and replaced the globe. She then reopened the bars and closed herself in.

Footsteps came toward her but then moved away. Lok opened the airlock, and a light shone through from the port side of the craft.

Aly creaked open her cell and stepped out. She peeked around the bulkhead toward Darius Lok at the bottom of the extended ramp, as he walked up to a trio of people—two men and one woman.

"Do you have it?" the woman in the middle asked him.

"It's nice to see you, too, Ravi," Lok shot back at her, putting his hand inside his jacket.

The two guards either side of Ravi cautiously moved their hands toward their sidearms. But their fears were allayed when Lok revealed a medical scanner. The same one Aly had found on the *Argo* before he'd knocked her out.

"As promised, DNA of the being known as Kione." He passed it to Ravi along with a small sample container.

Aly assumed he must have discovered some of the erroneous matter somewhere in the infirmary.

Ravi examined the data on the medical scanner. "This is good work, Darius."

"As always."

She rolled her eyes. "Yes, as always."

"Now, I'd like my payment, unless you have any other jobs for me."

"No, we're done here." She glanced at her two guards. "Pay him."

They unholstered their guns and Lok stumbled backward in shock. They then fired and Aly's captor fell, and his hole-ridden body slammed onto the deck with a thud.

Aly gasped but kept her eyes locked firmly outside the vessel.

Ravi walked over to him and inspected his corpse. "I'm sorry, Darius." She turned to her men. "Throw him back on his ship and blow it into space."

They nodded and dragged Lok with each arm toward *The Thor's Hammer*. Aly cowered behind the corner while they heaved his body beside her. Lok's open but very dead eyes stared up at her. She wanted to vomit but didn't dare.

One of Ravi's thugs pressed at the controls, and the ramp retracted. The airlock then clanged shut, leaving her in darkness. A few moments later, the sound of screeching metal echoed around her.

From her vantage point at the port side viewport, *The Thor's Hammer* blew outward toward the opened docking bay doors, hitting the sides with a thud on the way out into open space.

Aly banged against the bulkhead along with Lok's corpse. With the wind knocked out of her, she desperately pushed Lok's body away and dragged herself to her feet.

Up the ladder, she made her way to the cockpit and sat herself in the pilot's seat. Through the viewport was a moon as large as life, spinning like a top. Though in reality she knew it was *The Thor's Hammer* that was the object spinning out of control.

Aly checked over the helm controls, giving herself a crash course on the ship's systems. Lok's ship had two main thrusters and a set of maneuvering thrusters. She fired the latter and stopped the ship's spin.

She tried to pull up with the mains, but there was no power.

"Main thrusters are offline," the computer said in Lok's voice.

What a narcissist.

Aly assumed they must have been damaged from their sudden departure from the other ship.

"Now approaching atmosphere."

She fired the maneuvering thrusters again and made sure the heat shield pointed toward the moon. When the ship smashed into the outer atmospheric layer, everything around her reverberated as if *The Thor's Hammer* were being beaten with rocks.

If she didn't figure something out quickly, gravity would draw her to the surface.

I'm so going to die...

THIRTY-ONE

Serenity Science Station - Luna

Nora had been in Luna's orbit for over three hours. While they'd run every diagnostic imaginable on the piece of equipment, there was now the arduous task of repeating the process remotely via the main laboratory to ensure nothing went awry in transit. The last thing Javier wanted was for something to happen to it while in his possession. He valued his life too much, knowing Song would place the blame squarely on him.

He peered down at his console. The replicated Iota particles were holding steady with no apparent degradation.

Song walked over to him from an adjacent station. "The diagnostics are complete. We're ready when you are."

The butterflies in his stomach did flip-flops. It reminded him of the day as a much younger man when he'd waited for the first Mark IV trials to kick off. He turned to one of his assistants sitting at the workstation beside him. "Mister Tuhana, send a commlink to Pluto Station and inform them we're ready to begin our initial run."

On the large monitor of the rear wall of the laboratory, a visual image of Nora appeared. It was so small and insignificant up in Luna's orbit, but Javier knew if it was successful, the small piece of hardware would change everything.

A hush went up around the lab.

Javier nodded toward Professor Bennett, his head of Delivery Systems. "Activate the emitter."

"Activating," he replied.

Nora lit up blue, and her forward emitter glowed an ominous orange.

"Initialize the particle stream," Javier instructed him.

"Particle stream initialized."

Javier stood and checked the readings at Tuhana's station. All energy levels were within normal parameters, and the Iota particle delivery system was stable. "Coordinate check."

"Coordinates are locked in for two million kilometers outside Pluto's orbit," Tuhana replied.

It was the part Javier was most nervous about. To control the vortex from their end wouldn't be an issue, but it was a completely different proposition at the other. He hoped the exit point was far enough beyond the solar system's edge so it wouldn't create any issues.

"All right, let's see what Nora can do. Activate the particle stream."

Everyone's eyes focused on Nora as an orange beam of energy fired from her emitter toward the abyss. Javier gazed at Tuhana's monitor, checking over the indicators. The Iota particles rapidly emptied from Nora's storage system. Several more seconds passed, and the beam deactivated. Nora switched herself off, and she powered down.

Ahead of the device there was nothing but empty space.

"Report?" Javier asked Bennett.

"I'm picking up no change in readings on the scanners, Professor."

"What about the Iota particles?"

"They're decaying."

"Continue scanning. I want every piece of data we can get." Javier sighed and walked to Song's side. "How's Nora?"

She checked her monitors. "The emitter has minimal damage. By the time she fired off the last of the Iota particles, she shut herself down to stop any further issues."

"It's a nice failsafe to have."

She smirked. "Designed it myself."

"Professor!" Tuhana pointed to the main monitor.

A sparkle of light emerged at the particle bombardment point. Purple and red tendrils appeared, bounding against one another.

"A vortex!" Javier nudged his assistant from his seat

and studied the incoming data. "It's measuring two point one meters in diameter." He did a double take. "It's closing rapidly!"

"Launch the probe now!" Song instructed one of the other workstation operators on the other side of the lab.

The small test probe launched from Luna's surface and shot toward the vortex. The miniature craft was the smallest they had but regardless would be a tight squeeze. In the blink of an eye, the energy tendrils shimmered out and the probe continued racing at it and disappeared into nothingness.

Javier rubbed his sweaty palms together. "The probe's gone."

Song went to his side and peered over his shoulder at the readings. "Did it reach the vortex?"

Javier activated a commlink. "Pluto Station, do you read?"

"This is Pluto Station."

"Do you have a vortex on your end?"

A long silence followed, then an image appeared from the outlying facility on the monitor of the probe shooting out from the vortex, with the small planetoid of Pluto in the background.

"That's an affirmative, Professor."

A burst of applause rang out around the laboratory and Javier reached for his seat and sat down in shock. While the vortex was only small, and the corridor lasted mere seconds, it had worked. He was the first human to create a trans-space passageway.

"I've got to hand it to you, Javier." Song clutched his

shoulder and smiled in a way he'd never seen before. "Even I was impressed with that one."

Cargo Ship Argo

Conrad walked on to the bridge with a pair of coffee mugs in his hands. His colleague hadn't moved since he'd left. After sending out a system-wide alert for the whereabouts of *The Thor's Hammer*, Rycroft planted himself down at the operations station and fixed his eyeballs on the scanners and the comms.

Conrad handed him one of the mugs. "Anything?"

Rycroft shook his head, and Conrad sat at the helm, staring across at the captain's chair. He peered at the peeling upholstery of the center seat and lamented at how cursed it had become. He'd always sought to sit in it, and if everyone kept dying or leaving around him, he might have that chance.

But then there'd be no one left to give any orders to.

The pit of his stomach tightened. He'd been such an ass to Alyssa. He once would've given anything for the *Argo's* captaincy, but things had changed. He just wanted to see Rycroft get his daughter back.

"I remember what happened to her mother," Rycroft broke the silence. "I promised I'd never let anything happen to Alyssa. That I'd protect her. Now…"

"There comes a time when they grow up and you can't protect them anymore." Conrad thought of Tyler. The notion of him so far from home still boiled his blood.

"You might be right, but it doesn't make me feel any better."

Conrad took a sip of his coffee. "I know."

A faint crackling of static played over the speakers, with a muffled fizz of sound throughout it.

Rycroft toggled the controls and enhanced the audio. The fizz was a voice.

"That's Alyssa!" Conrad jumped from his seat and joined Rycroft's side.

"Can anyone hear me?" Aly's voice echoed from the bridge speakers. *"I'm dropping into the atmosphere of Io. My main thrusters are out. To anyone out there, please help!"*

Rycroft and Conrad stared at each other in unison. "Io!"

Conrad pointed at the scanners. "It'll take too long to get there."

Rycroft wore a steely gaze. "Not unless we punch the FTL." He hurried over to the helm and plugged in the calculations.

"FTL?" Conrad didn't need to remind Rycroft how stupid it was to use FTL inside a planet's gravitational field.

"I realize doing so will completely scramble our exit point and potentially throw us out somewhere we shouldn't be. But if we don't try this..."

Conrad nodded without a second thought and strapped himself into a chair. "Let's do it."

THIRTY-TWO

It wasn't the first time Kevin had used the *Argo's* FTL drive inside a planet's gravitational field, but it was the first time he'd done it so close to Jupiter and her dozens of moons. The Jovian system was a navigational nightmare. If he stuffed up, not only would he kill himself and Althaus, but there'd also be no one to rescue Alyssa.

He checked his calculations on the helm, ensuring they were accurate, and turned to Althaus. "Ready?"

His comrade nodded.

"Here goes." With a push of the lever, he blasted the *Argo* into FTL. Space bent before them, throwing the small cargo vessel beyond the speed of light.

In an instant, a sulfur dioxide haze replaced the twisted image of stars and the ship exploded from FTL straight into Io's atmosphere. The *Argo* rumbled violently around them.

"I guess that could've been worse!" Kevin yelled over the noise of the vessel being smashed about like an old wooden ship in a storm.

"It could've been better, too!" Althaus glanced at him, no doubt knowing they'd been just as lucky as he did.

Kevin gripped his console and pulled up. The *Argo* heaved through the volcanically charged vapors and roared upward into the moon's orbit.

"Can you see Aly?"

Althaus eyed his scanners. "There!" He ran his hands over his station and sent the coordinates to the helm.

Kevin plotted the course and skimmed the ship over the atmosphere until they reached her point of entry. "How far down is she?"

"Seven kilometers and dropping."

"We better get a move on." Kevin pushed at the controls and plunged the *Argo* downward. While Io didn't have a thick atmospheric layer, the many active volcanoes on its surface made it a nasty one to traverse.

Kevin activated a commlink. "Alyssa, can you read me?"

After a long silence a response rang out over the speakers. *"Dad!"*

Kevin's heart filled with warmth at his daughter's voice. "It's me, Alyssa. Hold on, we're on our way!"

The Thor's Hammer

Aly focused her eyes on the scanners. There was heavy interference, but the *Argo* was visible and powering toward her position. While she was excited to see her dad coming to the rescue, she kept her wits about her and did the math.

She reactivated her commlink. "I'm sorry to burst your bubble, but you won't reach me in time. At this point, I'll plunge headfirst into that giant group of volcanos beneath me before you catch up."

An awkward silence permeated on the other end of the channel. *"Don't worry, just hold on tight. We'll get you."*

Aly had heard that tone in her father's voice many times before. It was an attempt at being confident when he was anything but. She closed her eyes. She didn't want to die.

Think, Aly. Think.

I need more time.

With no way to launch upward with the main thrusters out, she needed to find another option.

The maneuvering thrusters!

Now she had someone to rescue her, she could make some seconds up with the less powerful thrusters. It wouldn't fire her into orbit but it would slow her descent. Maybe just enough for the *Argo* to grab her.

But I'll have to reroute all my main power.

She undid her harness and stumbled to the engine room in the craft's rear.

Cargo Ship Argo

"She's right. We'll just miss reaching her." Kevin bit his bottom lip. "Can we punch these thrusters any harder?"

Althaus shook his head. "They're running at maximum."

As they rocked about through the ferocious atmosphere, Kevin swore he saw the outline of *The Thor's Hammer*. It couldn't be. Aly was much farther down.

"Hold on a minute." Althaus perked up.

"What is it?"

"Her ship." He read from the scanners. "She's slowing."

"What?" Kevin looked down at his own console in disbelief, realizing what she'd done. "Damn, she's good. We'll make it. Prepare the grapple." He reactivated the commlink. "Stand by, Alyssa, we're going to attach. Keep your ventral thrusters to maximum, and I'll pull you to safety."

"Roger that!"

The *Argo*'s hull shuddered hard, lurching slightly off-kilter. Kevin darted his eyes at Althaus. "What the hell was that?"

"Bad news. Our thruster exhausts are getting clogged up with the atmospheric particulates. We're slowing."

"Will we still reach Alyssa in time?"

"Yes, but when we do, we'll have gone past the point of no return."

Kevin did a double take of the readings. Althaus was right. With the weight of *The Thor's Hammer* and the thrust available to them, they wouldn't be able to pull up in the required timeframe. Both Aly's ship and the *Argo* would go swimming inside a volcano.

Althaus unbuckled himself from his chair. "I may have an idea, however."

The Thor's Hammer

"You want me to do what!"

Aly bounded her way to the cockpit, disbelieving what her father had just suggested.

"We'll fire our grapple and attach to The Thor's Hammer. You'll have to leave the ship and ascend the grapple. Althaus will climb down it and meet you halfway to help you back aboard the Argo. Do you have an EV suit aboard?"

"Yeah." She remembered seeing one in the engine room.

"Kit up quickly."

Aly viewed the surface getting ever closer from the forward viewport and jumped from her seat.

I suppose if I die, it'll be one for the ages.

Cargo Ship Argo

Conrad opened the ventral airlock on the deck in the center of the cargo bay and jumped inside, kitted up in his clunky EV suit. He closed the door on top of him and pressed at the panel, depressurizing the small space.

"Are you ready down there, Althaus?" Rycroft said over the intercom.

Conrad checked the indicator, and the light blinked green. "Ready."

"All right, I'm firing the grapple now."

Conrad grabbed on to the handholds either side of him, and the *Argo* lurched, shooting the grapple downward.

"We have contact!"

"I'm opening the airlock." He latched his safety line from the suit to the inside of the compartment, and with a push of the button, opened the door.

He braced himself and, as expected, the oncoming storm of Io's atmosphere blasted and billowed around him. "I can't see a thing out here!"

He stepped out and felt around for the large tubular grapple extending from the *Argo*'s ventral hull. Like a child climbing down a tree, he went one foot at a time, all the while feeling as if he were being barraged with golf balls from an angry drunk at a driving range.

"Alyssa, can you hear me?" he asked over the commlink.

"I'm ascending now," she replied.

Conrad edged closer.

Through the din, an arm appeared. Assuming it wasn't some native inhabitant of Io not yet discovered, he put out his hand and grabbed it. He heaved her toward him and checked her over. Her suit was a wreck, and so would his soon if he didn't get them back.

He attached a safety line between the pair and held her tight. "Alyssa!"

She didn't respond and through her helmet her eyes were closed.

"Alyssa!"

"Rycroft, get us up now!" he yelled over the commlink.

The line wheeled them upward and inside the compartment. Both crashed hard into the bulkhead. Conrad mashed the panel to close the door and pressurize the small area.

Beneath them, the *Argo* retracted her grapple and pulled up beyond the atmosphere. Through the viewport, *The Thor's Hammer* continued to tumble downward to its molten tomb.

The compartment pressurized, and Conrad opened the airlock into the cargo bay. He hauled Alyssa onto the deck and tugged off her helmet.

She still didn't respond.

No!

He took off his own helmet and leaned in toward her, feeling a pulse on her wrist. She spluttered and her eyes burst open. Alyssa stared up at him in disbelief. Conrad immediately drew her in and gave her the biggest hug he'd ever given anybody in his life.

"I'm sorry," he said to her.

Her eyebrows rose in bewilderment, but she gave him a knowing look. She hugged him back and unlatched herself when her father bounded onto the deck from the elevator shaft.

"Don't hog her all to yourself." Rycroft put a thankful hand on Conrad's shoulder and bent down to give his daughter a loving embrace of his own.

THIRTY-THREE

Alpha Station

Jason gazed out the viewport at the numerous ships docked at Earth's main orbital facility. He hadn't seen an armada of its size since the war.

Captain Shila approached him from the door of the observation gallery. "Are you ready?"

He nodded, and they strolled out into the large circular wardroom of Alpha Station where the other captains and their executive officers were already mingling amongst themselves. As he walked past them, Jason got the same stares he'd received when he first arrived on the *Sabre's* command deck. He didn't know whether it was worse getting the same looks of disapproval from his superiors or the people below him in the chain of command.

He and Shila took a seat at their designated chairs around the large round table, just in time for Admiral

Mueller to arrive. The woman's aura immediately silenced them. She stood at the lectern at the head of the room, and activated the holographic projector above, while everyone sat. An image of a vortex appeared above their heads and a probe exited it and zoomed toward a planetoid.

"Three days ago, Professor Javier Petit of the Tokyo Institute of Advanced Sciences successfully tested a trans-space corridor between Luna and Pluto," Mueller began. "He borrowed a prototype known as Nora from the Vladivostok Project to make the test possible."

Jason smiled. For the first time since he'd heard the Destiny signal, there was now hope he could reach his brother.

"Petit has promised us a working trans-space actuator for deep space use." Mueller paused and regarded everyone around the room. "This morning the Ministry of Defense instructed me to put together an expeditionary force at full tactical readiness." She pulled up another image on the projector of a star chart magnified on a familiar section of space. "The Seeker weapon ship that was destroyed at Psi-Aion, sent a message here. That is our destination."

Jason's clenched his fists.

"While we're not sure what will be waiting for us here, the president wants us to use all our resources to find out." She tapped her hand against the lectern. "His instructions are for us to engage the Seekers."

Murmurs rang out around the wardroom, and Jason

glanced at Captain Shila. "This wasn't exactly how I thought my first mission back in the service would go."

Hopefully it won't be my last.

THIRTY-FOUR

Martian Tribune Building - Holden City, Mars

Marissa bounded out of the elevator and toward the reception desk of the main office.

Janine's eyes widened at the clock on the wall above her reception desk. "This is the third day this week you've been late. What gives?"

She wasn't being adversarial, but Marissa knew the receptionist suspected something was up. "A long story."

"If that man of yours is taking too much of your time, just send him to my place for the night." She licked her lips. "Janine will straighten him out for you."

Marissa wondered if it might not be such a bad idea. "I'll see what he says and get back to you."

Janine winked, and Marissa made her way into the bullpen where the *Tribune's* employees had gathered at the far end watching something on the large wall monitor.

"What's going on, Greg?" she asked one of her colleagues.

The older man didn't flinch. "Seems the president's making a special address."

On the monitor an image of President Jarret's lectern with the emblem of Caput Mundi House behind it appeared. The camera panned around, showing the bustling media room of journalists waiting for him to arrive. It then panned back to Patrick Ryland, Jarret's media advisor, striding onto the stage.

"Ladies and gentlemen, the President of the United Earth Commonwealth."

Ryland stepped aside, and President Jarret took his place at the center of attention. Behind him, an entourage followed. Among the ones Marissa recognized were his chief of staff, Luan Ntini, Minister of Defense Takashi, head of the trans-space project, Professor Petit, and CDF Admiral of Operations, Mueller.

"Earth has entered a new age," Jarret began. *"But that new age has presented us with challenges near and far. Fresh in our memories are the many fine men and women who lost their lives at Orion V. It was cold, calculated murder by a race of people who call themselves Seekers. A bloodthirsty species hell-bent on the destruction of all who stand in their way. If it weren't for the courageous acts of Commander Jason Cassidy and the crew of the* Cargo Ship Argo *destroying their superweapon, one can only wonder what predicament we might find ourselves in now."*

Jarret paused and stared out amongst the journalists

assembled. *"I've talked to the families of every single man, woman, and child who lost their lives. To them I've promised justice. To them I've promised an explanation for why their loved ones perished. That is why I've had Minister of Defense Takashi liaise with Admiral Mueller of the CDF to form an expeditionary force of a dozen vessels to find those answers. They will be equipped with our best diplomats and armed with our best soldiers."*

The bullpen of the *Martian Tribune* became a hive of activity as the swathes of reporters hurried to their cubicles to begin work on stories and get in contact with their people on the inside.

"Prior to the destruction of the Seeker vessels at Psi-Aion, one sent a message to a star a farther two hundred and eighty-three light-years away, in the Kappa-Magellan system. Our best experts don't know whether it was a call to their home world, a base, or something else. I have the greatest faith that our expeditionary force will find out."

An impatient young reporter sprang forth from her seat with a raised hand. *"How will the expeditionary force travel a journey of six hundred light-years with conventional FTL drives?"*

"That's a great question. To answer it, I present Professor Petit of the Tokyo Institute of Advanced Sciences."

Jarret gave up the lectern, and Petit took his place.

"With the technology my trans-space team has developed with the members of the Vladivostok Project on Luna, we've replicated the same trans-space corridors the

Argo *traveled through between Orion V and the Psi-Aion system."* Petit activated a holographic projector, and an image of a device appeared above him. *"A piece of hardware known as Nora will be installed on the flagship of the expeditionary force to open a trans-space corridor, allowing them to travel twenty-seven thousand times the speed of light. Six hundred and seventy-five times faster than our most advanced FTL drive."*

The press conference continued for another hour where Admiral Mueller detailed the makeup of the expeditionary force and the coming weeks of war games to sharpen the crew's skills. At its end, the last of the stragglers still listening at the *Tribune* raced back to their cubicles.

Marissa logged on to her computer, knowing she was in for a long day.

CDF Headquarters - Miami, Earth

Jason Cassidy rubbed his clammy hands against his knees. When Captain Shila gave him her blessing to see Admiral Mueller, he realized he wouldn't be in for an easy time.

Outside the admiral's office, the lieutenant behind the reception desk continued to look up from her work and stare at him. If it weren't for his situation, Jason would normally walk over and give her his commband number.

Hell, when has that ever mattered?

He stood and stepped toward her, but before he

could reach the desk, a hand touched his shoulder. "Admiral Foster!"

His old mentor smiled. "Welcome, Commander. They told me you have an appointment with Admiral Mueller. A bit presumptuous, aren't we?"

"I'm surprised she took my call at all." Jason chuckled.

"Come on, she's ready for you."

As he followed the admiral through, Jason winked at the lieutenant behind the reception desk. From inside, Admiral Mueller caught him in the act. She raised an eyebrow while she stirred her coffee, not breaking eye contact with him. Foster, not having seen anything, escorted him to the chairs at the front of the desk, and they both sat.

"Why are you here, Commander?" Mueller asked, getting straight to the point.

"I want to thank you for seeing—"

"Commander Cassidy, as you could well imagine, I'm a very busy woman. Captain Shila conveyed to me you wished to have a meeting. If it was anyone else, I would've told them to follow the chain of command. Luckily for you, I'm a kind and generous person."

Jason did his best not to laugh, not sure whether Mueller was joking or not. "Well, umm, the reason I'm here is to discuss the upcoming mission. The expeditionary force—"

"And?"

"Well, umm." He stopped and stared at Foster

whose eyes directed him to get on with it. "Admiral, I'm here to tell you how certifiably nuts this idea is."

Mueller didn't break her gaze with him.

"No one else in the CDF has dealt with the Seekers," Jason continued. "And while it appears I've been brought back into the service as a glorified poster boy to bring in new recruits, it wouldn't hurt the brass to hear my advice."

Mueller's eyes finally wavered, and she took a sip of her coffee. "I'm listening, Commander."

"If we're to send an expeditionary force to Seeker space, we might as well tell the crew to say their final goodbyes to their families now."

"You believe we'll fail?"

"To be blunt, Admiral, it's a suicide mission. No doubt you've read all the reports on these guys. We got lucky defeating them. The Seekers are killers, pure and simple."

"And that's the reason President Jarret wants to send this force. To see what we're up against."

"We already know what we're up against." Jason shook his head in frustration. "The real reason we're doing it is to deflect away from his crappy presidency."

"Do you believe the people who died deserve justice?"

Jason's mind turned to Tyler. He asked himself if he knew he was still deceased, would he think the same way. "The people who died are dead. They're not coming back. I understand that more than most, I assure you. But sending more people to die isn't the answer to that."

"So, you'd have us roll over." Mueller's hard-lined stare returned. "Appeasement has never been the answer."

"I don't disagree, but it's not that simple. We have no idea if the Seekers will come knocking on our door looking for revenge. But if we go out there and kick in the hornet's nest, we'll guarantee it. They'll open those trans-space vortexes of theirs and rain holy hell down on us." Jason waved at the beautiful Florida view out the window behind her. "You can forget about this. It'll be gone. All of it."

Mueller put her coffee cup down. "You must understand the decisions are made in offices much higher than this one."

"Then I would hope, Admiral, you would exploit your clout to make the people in those offices see sense."

She frowned. "Is there anything else, Commander?"

"There is. A request actually. I'd like to propose an alternate use for Nora."

"The trans-space actuator?"

Jason nodded. "Instead of waging interstellar war with it, let me use it to go to the Horizon Cluster and rescue my brother and Captain Marquez."

Mueller put up a hand. "Commander—"

"It was difficult to send rescue before. Now it's a whole new ballgame."

Mueller glanced at Foster and then back to Jason.

"I'll absorb everything you've told me today and see how far my clout takes me."

"That's all I ask, Admiral."

Jason stood and saluted, leaving her office behind, realizing it was likely the last time he'd get to see inside it.

THIRTY-FIVE

Tokyo, Earth

"Just like that?"

Jason stared out from the terrace of Doctor Tai's Tokyo apartment, not impressed with what Admiral Foster was telling him on the other end of the comm-link. "I wish I could say I was surprised."

"Admiral Mueller and I had a meeting at the Ministry of Defense in the afternoon," Foster said. *"They were rather equivocal in their stance that the mission go ahead."*

"Of course they were." Jason rolled his eyes. "So, I guess that means a no-go for my journey to the Horizon Cluster?"

"TIAS have informed us it'll take three months to build another trans-space actuator to the required specifications. Should the expeditionary force not require it, Minister Takashi has promised he will consider it for use in the rescue of your brother and Captain Marquez."

"By that stage I'll be dead somewhere out in Seeker territory." Jason shook his head. "I'm sorry, Admiral, I realize you tried."

"We'll talk soon, Commander. Foster out."

Jason deactivated his commband and opened the glass door. He strolled into the living area of the apartment where Tai and Petit were sitting across from each other in quiet conversation.

"I apologize," Jason said to them. "I forgot how problematic it was dealing with the brass."

"Anything we can help with?" Petit asked.

"I'm curious, how long will it take you to build another Nora?"

"I've projected three months."

"Well, I guess they weren't lying about that."

Petit raised an eyebrow.

"Don't worry, Professor. I'll sort out my own problems." Jason sat beside them. "Now tell me, what can I do for you?"

"We've tracked down where Kione is," Tai said.

It was the first bit of good news Jason had heard for some time. "Where?"

"A secure facility in Edinburgh. They've put him under the supervision of a Doctor Charles Whitlowe."

"What's so special about this Whitlowe guy?"

"I have no idea. I can't find out one shred of information about him."

"That's worrying."

"It's as if he doesn't exist. He's not a part of any medical association throughout the commonwealth, and after contacting everyone I know, no one else has heard of him either."

"What about Kione?" Jason asked. "How is he?"

Tai looked to Petit before turning back to Jason. "When I got to sit down with him..."

"What?"

"Something wasn't right. They drugged him. I'm sure of it." She bit her lower lip. "And when the meeting ended, he touched me. For a moment it seemed he contacted me—mentally."

Jason remembered back to his time incarcerated on the Seeker weapon ship and the experience he'd shared with Kione. It was still so vivid in his mind. "But how? There's no sphere."

"I'm not sure."

"What did you see?"

"He was screaming out." Tai took a breath. "He wanted my help."

Jason rubbed his forehead. In that moment he was ashamed of humanity. He'd rescued Kione from the Seekers just to hand him back to monsters of the same ilk.

"There is a segment of the media pushing to know what happened to Kione on his return from Outpost Watchtower," Petit added.

"All of which is being drowned out by the news of Jarret's expeditionary force." Jason stood and walked to the window.

"We could reach out to them. Tell them what we—"

Jason shook his head. "They won't let this get out, Professor. Even if it did, a part of the community blames him for what happened at Orion V, so he wouldn't be safe. The xenophobic fires have well and truly been stoked."

"Then what's your suggestion?"

"Let's see if we can find something out about this Whitlowe character to start with. I know a guy. That's if he's still alive." Jason's commband alerted him to an incoming commlink. "Cassidy here."

"This is Captain Shila. Commander, I need you to report to the Sabre*."*

"Captain, I—"

"That's now, Commander."

Jason sighed. "On my way."

He turned apologetically to Tai and Petit. "I'll give you this guy's name. It's somewhere to start at least."

UECS Sabre

Jason stepped onto the command deck where Captain Shila signed off a data tablet and handed it to a junior officer. She spotted Jason and motioned him to her office. He walked in and stood in front of her desk. But instead of taking a seat behind it, Shila gestured to the two sofa-style chairs in the corner.

"Sit down, Jason."

Jason? She'd never been so informal. *What have I done wrong?*

"There's no easy way to tell you this, but it's about the *Argo*," she said to him.

His chest tightened. "What—"

"Six hours ago, Ganymede Station detected the cargo ship on an irregular course. They sent out a pod to investigate. Her thrusters were firing erratically, so they boarded her and got her under control." She gazed deep into his eyes. "They found no one aboard."

Jason stared blankly out the viewport. "When you say no one aboard—"

"There were no bodies. No airlocks were blown."

"So someone has taken them?"

"That's what the authorities on Ganymede Station believe. However, at this point they've turned up nothing giving them a definite answer or their potential whereabouts."

"And the *Argo*?"

"It's at Ganymede Station. They're going over it with a fine-tooth comb as we speak."

Doctor Tai once asked Jason how many lives he had, but in truth it was the *Argo* that had the fortunate luck. As its crew kept dying or disappearing, the humble old cargo ship continued to survive. It would almost be funny if it weren't for the fact his friends were missing.

"Captain, I realize I have no leave clocked up yet, but I'll need to take some time to sort this out," Jason pleaded. "With these war games coming up, I'm sure it'll piss off the brass but—"

"I'll take care of them," Shila said, stopping him in his tracks. "Go to Ganymede and find your friends."

Jason smiled as best he could in the circumstances. His new captain was quickly rocketing up his list of favorite people.

THIRTY-SIX

Transport Pod

It'd been years since Jason had passed through the Jovian system of moons. While very much a part of humanity's home, it'd always appeared so alien to him. Centuries after Earth's first unmanned probes traveled through, many still regarded it a mysterious expanse of the abyss.

His transport approached the Ganymede moon and its orbiting station. During his voyage he'd barely got a wink of sleep. However, when he had, he always dreamed of Aly and Kevin. Even Althaus popped in from time to time, which was a little disconcerting.

"Stand by for landing, everyone," the pilot announced over the speakers.

The pod made a beeline for the hangar deck of Ganymede Station and touched down. Through the crowd of other passengers, Jason's welcoming committee declared itself in the form of a weedy-looking young man.

"Commander Jason Cassidy," he greeted him, no doubt recognizing his CDF uniform as it was the only one amongst the other passengers. "I'm Detective Marcetti."

Jason wondered if the kid was still popping pimples. "This isn't your first case, is it?"

Marcetti bristled but ignored the comment. "Come with me, Commander."

Jason frowned and followed him from the hangar deck into the central administration hub. "What can you tell me so far, Detective?"

Marcetti led him up a flight of stairs into a fanatically tidy office and flicked on a wall monitor behind his small desk. "The *Cargo Ship Argo* arrived at Ganymede Station on May twenty-first to drop off a consignment of medical supplies." He brought up a timetable of their arrival, the cargo manifests, and images of their landing on the hangar deck. "Later that night, Kevin Rycroft reported his daughter missing."

"Wait." Jason hadn't heard that part of the story. "What happened to Aly?"

"Kevin Rycroft and Conrad Althaus returned to the ship and found Alyssa gone. Surveillance cameras showed signs of tampering. I've since discovered both men visited one of Ganymede Station's computer technicians and beat a confession out of him. Seems a person by the name of Darius Lok paid him off to alter the footage during the time Miss Rycroft went missing."

"What happened next?"

"Darius Lok's ship, *The Thor's Hammer,* logged a flight plan to Europa Station. The *Argo* followed sometime later, but Lok's vessel never arrived."

"He'd filed a dummy flight plan?"

"Correct." Marcetti revealed a scanning log. "The last sighting of the *Argo* was her leaving Europa Station heading toward Io."

"Io?" Jason pondered. "Something must've led them there."

"I came to the same conclusion and sent a pod out there to investigate. Unfortunately, nothing so far has come up."

"So, that's where we're at?"

Marcetti nodded. "I'm still following up on a few leads, but I believe concentrating on Io is our best bet at this stage."

"Very well. I think it's time I had a look at the *Argo*."

"She's in the hangar deck."

Jason walked to the exit but then stopped and turned. "Hey."

"Yeah?"

"What I said earlier, I didn't mean to be an ass. I just..." He trailed off. "You've done good work."

Marcetti nodded, and Jason headed to the hangar deck where he boarded the *Argo*. He searched throughout the empty cargo bay for any clues, followed by everyone's quarters. From the frugalness of Kevin's room, to the messiness of Aly's, and then finally to the downright smelliness of Althaus's. Nothing seemed out of place.

Up on A Deck, he explored the engine room, the galley, the infirmary, and even the rec room. All the pieces on the chessboard were in their starting positions as if no one had ever lived there. He grabbed the board and threw it into the bulkhead.

The pieces clattered over the deck.

He made his way to the bridge through the hatchway. Like the rest of the ship, it was eerily quiet. Jason stared at the empty chairs and sat at the helm.

He put his head in his hands in hopelessness.

An alert beeped on the console. *"DNA detected,"* the computer chirped. *"Cassidy, Jason Benjamin."*

He opened his eyes, and the lights blinked off, bathing him in darkness.

"Hello, Mister Cassidy."

"What the..." Jason jumped from his seat at the female voice and peered around the bridge. But no one was there.

"Up here."

He glanced at the speakers, realizing someone was communicating across a commlink. "Who is this?"

"Who I am is irrelevant."

Jason hastened over to the operations station and checked the comms.

"I assure you, you'll be unable to trace this commlink."

That didn't stop Jason from trying. Though he quickly realized she was right.

"I need you to listen carefully."

"Seems I have little choice."

"We have an opportunity to help each other, Mister Cassidy. There's something I require. In exchange, I'll return the crew of the Argo *to you."*

"What have you done to them!" Jason clenched his fist. "I swear, if you've harmed—"

"Mister Cassidy, getting emotional will only hinder the situation. Now listen. One week ago, an associate boarded your vessel in the hope of retrieving a DNA sample of the life form known as Kione."

Jason furrowed his brow, remembering what Marcetti had told him. *Darius Lok...*

"He retrieved the DNA, but our scientists deemed it unfeasible for use. Luckily for us, our associate brought aboard the Argo's *captain."*

"Aly?"

"After her crewmates rescued her, we took all three captive." The woman cleared her throat. *"This is where you come in, Mister Cassidy."*

Jason gritted his teeth. "I want to see them!"

On the operations station, an image of the three sitting together in a holding cell appeared. He put his hand on the monitor, as if trying to reach out to them.

"As you can tell, they're uninjured and being taken care of. However, that could change..."

"What do you want?" Jason asked.

"That's the spirit, Mister Cassidy. Now, since the last DNA sample of Kione wasn't up to scratch, we would prefer the real thing."

"You want me to get you Kione? What do you want with him anyway?"

"That's ir—"

"Irrelevant. Right." He rolled his eyes. "How do you expect me to get him?"

"That's not my problem. I know you're very resourceful and will find a way."

The image of Aly, Kevin, and Althaus was replaced with a star chart. Prominent were the inner planets of the solar system. Crosshairs singled out a point in space beyond the orbit of Luna.

"Once you've retrieved Kione, I'll be waiting here. You have ten days."

"Ten days! How do you expect me—"

"Any funny business, and your people die. Do you understand?"

Jason sighed. "Understood."

The star chart disappeared, and the bridge lights came back on. A few moments later, Detective Marcetti arrived through the hatchway.

"What happened?" he asked. "The rear entry ramp wouldn't open. It's like the whole ship powered down."

Jason moved to the helm and began his preflight checks. "How soon can I get clearance out of here?"

THIRTY-SEVEN

Edinburgh, Earth

Doctor Charles Whitlowe stood before the monitor watching over Kione inside his bio-chamber. The alien being was unconscious, but his body shuddered from top to bottom at the energy bombarding it. He shook his head at the readings. He'd been working with Kione for over two weeks, and his methods were still no closer to bringing the extraterrestrial's abilities to the surface.

"Shut it down!"

Charles's assistant, Le Favre, flicked at the controls and deactivated the bio-chamber. While Kione's life signs weren't as stable as normal, they were still within normal parameters.

"Do you want me to get him out of there, Doctor?" Le Favre asked.

Charles nodded at her, and three of his assistants hurried into the medical bay to retrieve him. They placed his unconscious body onto a mobile stretcher and took him back to his quarters.

"Doctor Whitlowe, there's a call coming in for you."

Charles smacked the intercom on the console with his fist. "Who is it?"

"Minister Takashi."

He closed his eyes in frustration. "Send it down here." He put on the cheeriest expression he could muster, and the monitor filled with the face of the commonwealth's Minister of Defense. "Minister Takashi, so good to see you."

The man had heavy eyelids, portraying someone who'd had little sleep. *"What have you got to report, Whitlowe?"*

"I just finished another experiment, and while the results weren't what I was expecting, I am getting closer to the desired outcome."

"In other words, you lucked out again and have nothing to show for it?"

"I wouldn't put it quite that way Minister, I—"

"Whitlowe, you've had weeks on this. You guaranteed us you were the person for the job. The president has my balls in a vice. You of all people should know when you get on his wrong side what he's capable of." Takashi leaned in. *"Now listen closely. I'll call you back in a week. If I'm not informed of any progress, I'll recommend to Jarret you be pulled from the project and Kione be returned to TIAS."*

Before Charles could say a word, the screen went blank. He sat down in the nearest chair and tapped his fingers on the workbench. There was only one option left in his arsenal.

Using it, however, might mean risking Kione's life...

Martian Tribune Building - Holden City, Mars

Marissa popped two aspirin and guzzled down an entire glass of water. She closed her eyes and massaged her temples. The brightness of her computer monitor made her want to vomit, and the commotion in the surrounding bullpen rang in her head like a bell. She did her best to refocus her attention on a piece on the commanding officers of the expeditionary force. It was tedious to write, and she feared it would be even worse to read.

On the cubicle wall was a photo of Marcus and her on vacation at Planitia Resort, a year earlier. She smiled at how much simpler things had been back then.

But why are they so different now?

"Hey, are you coming out to lunch today?"

She glanced up at Evan Gray, one of the *Tribune's* leading sports reporters.

"Me and Li Jun booked a table at the new Italian restaurant down on Fifth Street," he said.

The thought of it made her want to vomit again. "Enjoy yourselves. I'll stick around here."

"When do you ever say no to Italian?"

"When I have work to do."

Evan peered over her shoulder and scoffed. "What are you trying to do, put our readers asleep?"

She glared at him.

"Sorry," he said, putting his hands up.

"You two go." Marissa peeked over the top of her cubicle at Li Jun sipping a coffee at the other end of the bullpen. "I know you've wanted to get her alone for a while."

His eyes darted either side of him, and he leaned in toward her. "Do you mind not broadcasting that?"

"Just ask her out, for crying out loud. She won't bite."

"And if she does?"

Marissa rolled her eyes. "You're so weak."

The *Tribune's* editor, Sandra Veroni, approached them. "You two look suspicious. What's going on?"

"Nothing!" Evan said in a high-pitched voice.

"I was just telling him he should ask Li Jun out," Marissa informed her.

Sandra glanced over at the younger female reporter. "I think that's a great idea."

Evan's face went red, and Sandra and Marissa laughed, watching him retreat to his cubicle.

"Can I see you in my office?" Sandra asked, her demeanor becoming a little more serious.

Marissa nodded, closing her computer down and following Sandra through the bullpen.

"Close the door," her editor instructed her.

Marissa did so and sat in front of the desk.

"Is everything all right?" Sandra asked.

The two had mended their working relationship since she'd gone over her editor's head with the Orion V story, and Marissa hadn't expected such a blunt question to begin their meeting. "I'm not sure what you mean."

Sandra spun her computer around. It was an article Marissa had written earlier in the morning about a police shooting on the west side of the city.

"While your story's on point, it's full of mistakes. It's as if a college freshman wrote it. Hell, when I verified it with the police department, they told me you got the names of the detectives and the victims around the wrong way."

Marissa narrowed her eyes and read over the soup of words in front of her. Sandra was right. She smiled apologetically.

"If this was a one-off, I wouldn't be worried." Sandra swiveled the computer around. "But I've noted numerous gaps in a lot of your work lately. Since you got back from Earth, it's as if your mind's been somewhere else."

"I'm not sure what to say."

"Have you become bored? When you break the biggest story of your career, the work afterwards can seem almost menial in comparison." Sandra stood and walked over to a glass case in the corner. She pulled out a small trophy. "I won this for an exclusive I wrote on a scandal in the supreme court fifteen years ago. I never came close to repeating anything else like it."

Marissa hadn't thought of that. The notion she may never break another big story scared her. "I guess I'm exhausted. It's been a long six months."

Sandra frowned. "Well, normally I'd tell you to take the week off and come back fresh, but the bigwigs upstairs have another assignment for you."

Marissa furrowed her brow.

Sandra returned the award inside the case and closed it. "With the CDF expeditionary force coming together, they want you to head up our coverage of the war games."

"Go back to Earth?"

"If you're not up to it, I'll send someone else. You can have leave. Take a month if you'd like. Michael could do the coverage."

"No." While Marissa liked the idea of time off, as a professional she couldn't say no to the opportunity. "I'll do it." She'd developed a standing at the *Tribune* and wouldn't be knocked off her pedestal.

Sandra sat back down. "I knew you'd say that. I had to try, I guess."

"Thank you for trying." Marissa stood and made her way to the door.

"Oh, Marissa!"

She turned.

"When you go to Earth, see if you can find what you lost. Those bigwigs upstairs, they won't remember the big stories forever."

Holden City, Mars

Marissa closed the front door as softly as possible and kicked her shoes into the corner. There was a distinct smell of spaghetti sauce in the air.

What is everyone's obsession with Italian at the moment?

She walked down the hall into the kitchen to find Marcus stirring a hot pot of food.

"This has to be a record." He checked his watch. "I can't remember the last time you were home when the sun was still up."

Once it would have been a jovial quip. Now there was a thin hint of sarcasm in his voice.

Marissa put her bag on the kitchen counter. "Sandra let me out of the asylum early."

"Well, isn't that nice of her?" Marcus took the wooden spoon from the pot and placed it in the sink. In another bowl he'd prepared a large serving of fresh pasta.

"There's something I have to tell you." She stepped closer and rested her hand beside him.

"Yes?"

"Work are sending me back to Earth to cover the war games."

Marcus put the pasta in two bowls and poured a healthy serving of sauce on each. There wasn't even the slightest hint of emotion on his face.

"Are you going to say something?" she asked him.

"What do you want me to say?"

"I'm not sure. Something. Anything."

He grabbed a pair of forks from the drawer and nestled one beside each bowl. "When we got together, I knew what I was getting into with your job. I understood there'd be early mornings and late nights. And I realized you'd have to travel. I've accepted that. If you need to go to Earth, that's fine."

It frustrated Marissa how calm he was. "Then what is it? What's happened between us?"

"Only you can answer that, Marissa. I'm not the one who brought baggage back with me." He walked to the fridge and pulled a jar of parmesan from it.

"You're the second person today who's said something along those lines."

The doorbell rang, and Marcus brushed past her down the hall. She placed a liberal amount of cheese on her dish and dug into her bowl. The murmurs at the front door echoed through to the kitchen, though she couldn't understand what was being said.

Footsteps came up the hallway.

"Marissa, this gentleman says he knows you."

She turned to Marcus's voice with a mouthful of pasta, and a figure stepped out from behind him.

She put down her bowl and nearly choked on her food.

"Jason!"

THIRTY-EIGHT

"What are you doing here?" Marissa said through her mouthful of food.

Jason wanted to tease her about catching her off guard, but it wasn't the time. "I need your assistance."

She finished the last remnants of her meal and placed it on the kitchen counter. "What for?"

Marcus stood between the pair appearing to weigh Jason up. Marissa noticed and put a hand around her partner's waist.

"Can you give us a moment?" she asked him.

He looked back at Jason and then at her. Without any protest, he picked up his bowl of pasta and strolled off into the living area.

Marissa grabbed Jason by the arm and dragged him out onto the balcony of her apartment, closing the screen door behind her. "You came to my house?" she snapped venomously.

"I'm sorry. I tried you at your office, and they told

me you'd gone home early for the day." He put his hands on the railing. "I wouldn't have come unless it was necessary."

She crossed her arms. "What do you need?"

Jason gazed out at the sun falling over the Martian horizon. "Someone has taken my crew from the *Argo* hostage."

"Wait. What!"

He filled her in on everything that'd happened since Captain Shila had given him permission to go to Ganymede Station, along with all he'd found out when he was there.

"Jesus, you've got yourself into some serious trouble, Jason," she said.

"Not as much as Aly, Kevin, and Althaus are in."

"I'm flattered you came to me, but I'm not sure how I can—"

"I've done some digging on this Darius Lok guy." Jason stepped closer to her. "From what I found out, going through ship registration records, Lok is an alias for Julian Perry. He was born and raised in Holden City, right here on Mars."

"I guess someone's got to start somewhere." Marissa bit her bottom lip. "And you think I can help you with that?"

"Well, believe it or not, while I didn't have a subscription to the *Martian Tribune*, I had time to read your articles occasionally. And when you'd started with the paper, I remember you did a lot of work in the crime pages. Most of your stuff was on the gangland war between the Petrellos and the Gallaghers. So I figured—"

"I'd have contacts?"

"Yeah."

"That was a long time ago, Jason. By the end of those street wars, there was barely anyone left of those families who didn't end up either dead or in jail."

"A few cockroaches always survive."

Marissa rubbed her chin. "There might be someone."

Jason smiled. "I knew I came to the right place."

"Don't thank me yet. There are never certainties in life on the red sands."

The pair stood on the balcony and watched the sun drop over the horizon, as the great dome of Holden City turned to darkness. If it were any other time or place, Jason would've thought he were in Heaven, but he couldn't get the images of Aly, Kevin, and Althaus from his mind. And he wouldn't until he'd finally freed them.

"They don't call it the wrong side of the tracks for nothing, do they?"

Jason stared out from the passenger side of the hovercar while Marissa drove down the less affluent streets of Holden City.

"Some of these buildings are among the first that sprang up when the original colony was founded," she said.

"No kidding. Half of them are falling apart."

"Most are government housing for the poor. There are some that house four generations of the same family."

"Generational poverty..." Jason shook his head. "You'd think when we left Earth we'd have learned from our past."

"Our technology might be better than anytime in human history, but society still treat the poorest of people as an infestation." Marissa stopped at an intersection and then turned right. "Greed continues to reign supreme. And because of it, places like this exist. Not to mention the crime that comes with it."

Jason had seen similar on Odyssey Station during his time there. He'd wondered now that Professor Petit had harnessed trans-space technology what they'd find in the great beyond. Would they discover more worlds like Psi-Aion and Earth? Perhaps they'd discover planets more advanced where humans would seem just as primitive as the people of Psi-Aion.

That's if we get that far and aren't exterminated by the Seekers.

"How have you been anyway?" Jason asked.

"Fine," she answered a little too quickly.

Even after all these years he remembered her expression when she didn't want to talk. After their rendezvous at the Sierra Nevada Mountains, she'd made it abundantly clear that what'd happened was something that could never be spoken of again. He couldn't blame her. She had everything. The perfect life. Her dream job. A beautiful apartment overlooking the city. And Marcus seemed like a stand-up guy.

Marissa directed the car down a side street which took them on to another main road and then their final destination. "Here we are. The largest maximum-security prison on Mars. Home to the worst Holden City has to offer."

She pulled into the visitor entrance, and they got out and made their way into the primary building.

"How did you get us in here again?" Jason asked her while they walked into the small room.

"You need to have connections." Marissa sat at one of the many tables.

Jason took the seat beside her, and the door opposite them opened, revealing the large hulking mass of Taz McPhee. "That guy belongs on a football field!"

"Shh." Marissa glared at him.

"Marissa Caldwell," Taz said in a high-pitched voice, completely betraying his massive size. "Or has it changed?" He stared down at her wedding finger. "You're still on the market? I'm out of here in seven years. If you can wait—"

The two prison guards behind him pushed him down into his chair and chained his cuffs to the table. Marissa nodded at them, and they left the three alone.

"How are you, Taz?" Marissa asked him.

"I'm in jail." He shrugged and turned to Jason. "Who are you?"

"He's a friend."

"He got no tongue?"

"I've got a tongue," Jason said. "My name's irrelevant. Makes things less messy."

"I guess I can understand that."

Jason put his hands on the table and leaned in toward him. "Marissa tells me you got her some information during the gangland wars."

"I may have."

"She also told me you ended up in here with a reduced sentence because you informed on your employers."

"It seemed the right thing to do."

"Well, I'm looking for info of my own."

"I'm out of that business now." McPhee smirked. "Unless it gets me less time in here?"

"That's something we can't offer," Marissa said.

"This would be on the down-low. No cop involvement," Jason told him.

The crim bit his bottom lip. "Sounds like my kind of thing, but as I told you, I shut up shop long ago."

Marissa put her hands on his, caressing the man's large tattooed hand. Jason did his best not to vomit.

"Come on, Taz, you need to take care of yourself in retirement. You said yourself, you'll be out in seven years. Do you still have that bank account?"

He nodded.

"Well, my friend is after a name. That's all. I'm sure he'd be willing to part with some money you can spend on a party when you're released."

McPhee gave her a cheeky grin. "Will you be there?"

"We'll see."

He turned to Jason. "What are you after?"

"Information on a man named Darius Lok," Jason said.

"Never heard of him."

He pulled out a small photo. "What about Julian Perry?"

McPhee narrowed his eyes and tapped his fingers on the table. "Yeah, I recognize him."

"I need to know who his employer is?"

"When I knew him, he worked with the Gallaghers. Looked like a sissy with all that flowing hair. Bit of a buffoon, but he got the job done most of the time. He left before the gangland wars ended to ply his trade off-world."

"Who did he go on to work for?"

"He's a bounty hunter. He had several employers."

"I'm after one who's extremely cashed up. One who thrives on the biggest of jobs."

McPhee smiled, revealing his set of black and broken teeth. "Ten thousand credits."

Jason did the arithmetic of his bank balance in his head. "Five thousand."

"This isn't a negotiation. It's ten thousand or I call the guards and I go back to my cell. Do you want your name or not?"

"Ten thousand it is," Marissa said. "I'll cover the rest."

McPhee seemed equally bemused, and he glanced at Jason. "Maybe you should be the one putting a ring on her finger."

Jason stared at her in shock and returned his attention to McPhee. "I want that name."

THIRTY-NINE

UECS Sabre

Captain Shila was the first to greet Jason when he returned aboard. "It's good to have you back, Commander."

He stepped out of the airlock of the transport pod onto the hangar deck. "I hope you haven't missed me too much?"

"We managed." Shila led him out into the corridor. "There's a representative from Intel waiting in the briefing room, so I assume you have news?"

Jason nodded. "With what I discovered aboard the *Argo* and some sleuthing on Mars, I got on the horn to the people at Intel. They believe the crew of the *Argo* are being held hostage by an individual by the name of Ravi Trentham."

"What does she want with them?"

"Kione."

They entered the elevator and ascended through the ship.

"Do you know why?"

"No, but it can't be for anything good."

The elevator came to a halt, and they walked out and headed toward the briefing room. They found a man in plain, nondescript civilian attire standing by the wall monitor when they entered.

"Commander Cassidy, this is Agent Moss from Intelligence," Shila introduced them.

Moss shook his hand. "We talked over many commlinks. It's good to meet you in person, Commander."

Jason gestured at the monitor. "What have you found on Ravi Trentham?"

"She's one of the most notorious and richest underworld figures in the solar system." Moss activated his presentation, producing an image of Trentham. The woman had long, dark-brown hair and hazel eyes. "While little more than a minor player only a decade ago, she made considerable financial gains during the Earth-Centauri War. From there she built up her holdings, and with the collapse of the McKinley family's slice of the pie here, she bulldozed all that stood before her. Her legitimate businesses include manufacturing on Luna and Mars, a transport business based around Saturn, and several casinos throughout the asteroid belt. While not proven, it's assumed she also distributes weapons and drugs on the black market."

"Sounds like a nasty customer," Shila said. "Any idea what she'd want with the alien?"

"No." Moss shook his head. "Despite what we have on her, she runs a tight ship. She's incredibly secretive and rarely comes out in public. We've been trying to plant a mole in her organization for years. But to date we've had little luck."

Jason rubbed his chin, forgetting there was no longer a beard there. "The question is, can we be sure she's the one responsible for taking the crew of the *Argo*?"

Moss pulled up a large swath of scanning data. "With the help of the stations surrounding Jupiter, I've overlaid scanning radiuses from every facility."

Jason did a double take at what looked like an impressive group of Venn diagrams surrounding the gas giant.

Moss pointed. "On the date of May twenty-second, a ship running dark was spotted traveling to Io. It rendezvoused with another vessel we believe to be *The Thor's Hammer*."

"Darius Lok..." Jason figured.

"Right. After a brief meeting, the unknown vessel disposed of Lok's ship and sent it hurtling into Io's atmosphere. Soon after, the *Argo* came along. Seems Alyssa Rycroft got a distress call out in time and her crewmates rescued her. When the *Argo* set a course for Ganymede Station, our unknown vessel turned around and headed back in their direction."

It all played out in front of them on the monitor until the two vessels disappeared in a scanning black spot. More time passed, and the unknown ship returned from the shadows, without the *Argo*, before disappearing for good beyond the region.

"It wasn't until several days later that the *Argo* showed up on Ganymede Station's scanners, adrift and crewless," Moss continued. "This is where we believe they were kidnapped."

Jason narrowed his eyes. "Okay, but this unknown ship of yours disappears once it leaves the Jovian system of moons. How can you tell it was Trentham's if it was running dark?"

Moss brought up a hazy magnified image of a craft against the backdrop of Jupiter. "Because a passing freighter took a visual scan, albeit a little crude."

Moss pressed in the terminal, and a second, much clearer ship appeared next to it. "This was found approaching Ceres two days later."

"It's the same ship." Jason stepped closer to the monitor. "Ravi's vessel?"

"My people on the ground on Ceres saw an increase of activity at her casino when it arrived in orbit. And piecing together the information you provided of the *Argo* crew in their cell, we've come to the conclusion they're being held near the major safe three levels beneath the surface."

"You've been able to pinpoint their exact position?" Shila asked.

"We believe so." Moss turned off the monitor. "A team is deployed and ready to go in."

While Jason would have preferred to do it a different way, he realized there was little choice. They couldn't hand Kione over, and if they tried to negotiate, it would blow their chance of catching Trentham off guard. "Very well. But I'm coming with you."

New York City, Earth

Susan directed her wheelchair through the lobby of the grungy old apartment building. Noting the cracked walls, she wondered how long the structure had left before it crumbled in a heap. Even the elevator was from another time. She half expected there to be a bellboy to help her. With great difficulty, she reached up and pushed the button for the eighth floor.

The gates closed, and she headed upward ever so slowly. At the top, she moved down the dark corridor, thanking her lucky stars her feet didn't make contact with the manky two hundred-year-old carpet. She followed the door numbers until she found apartment she 8K.

Susan knocked, but no one replied. "Mister Groth. My name's Doctor Susan Tai. It's taken a long time to find you. I'm in desperate need of help!"

Still no response.

All this way for nothing.

It'd been over a week since she'd seen Kione.

What must he be going through?

She banged on the door with more force. "Jason Cassidy sent me. He told me you knew his father!"

Footsteps finally approached from the other side, and the unlatching of several locks sounded. The door swung open, revealing a very old and very unwell man. His clothes were tattered, and the stench of his home was a combination of mold, bleach, and urine.

"Benjamin Cassidy. You know him?" he asked with a raspy voice.

She shook her head. "No, sir. I know his son. Benjamin Cassidy is dead."

Groth looked away, trying to hide his distress. "What about Althaus?"

"Conrad Althaus? He's still alive," she told him.

"A pity," he grumbled and waved her inside. "What can I help you with?"

She followed him into his apartment, just scraping her wheelchair through the doorway. The inner sanctum was full of darkness with the odd sliver of light peeking through the closed windows. Books and old newspapers were scattered over the floor, and on the walls were unusual paintings, from landscapes to portraits, and some things she couldn't identify.

"Jason told me you used to be in law enforcement," Susan said. "You cut your teeth as a composite artist."

Groth raised his eyebrows. "That was a long time ago."

"I'm trying to find the true identity of a person. If you can help me sketch him out..."

He rummaged on the floor and pulled out a fresh canvas. He put it on a stand and grabbed a brush and some paint. "Describe his eyes to me."

Over the next hour, the pair went back and forth until the portrait came out how Susan wanted.

"Incredible." She gazed at the drawing. "That's Doctor Whitlowe."

Groth yanked a small device from his pocket and motioned it over the images. He took a blanket off a nearby computer and blew the dust from it. He placed the device on the terminal, and it captured his painting on the monitor.

Susan moved to his side and Groth's hands danced over the keypad with remarkable speed for someone of his age and condition. A scrolling list of names appeared, and the computer started its search.

"This is a government database. How do you have access to it?" she asked.

"It's best you don't ask."

The computer continued until an image emerged.

"Is that him?" Groth asked.

"That's him." Susan recognized his eyes. "He's younger, though."

"This was taken six years ago," he read from the data. "The last photo on record."

"Can you open his file?"

Groth attempted to do so, but large red text filled the monitor: SEALED.

"Seems like this Doctor Whitlowe has a secret to keep. His file is sealed by presidential order." Groth put his hands back on the keypad. "No matter."

The red text disappeared, and his summary opened.

Susan furrowed her brow. "How did you—?"

He glanced at her with knowing eyes.

"Right. Don't ask."

"This man is no Doctor Whitlowe," he read. "His real name is William Ramsey. He was an extractions officer for Intel during the war."

"An extractions officer?"

"Mister Ramsey would've been in charge of high-level enemy soldiers after they were captured. Put plainly, Doctor Tai, he was a torturer."

The pit of Susan's stomach clenched.

"And going off his record," Groth continued, "he had some very harsh methods and was quite successful at his job."

She dropped her head. It was now more important than ever to get Kione out.

But how?

FORTY

Edinburgh, Earth

Charles hadn't attempted anything like it since the war. He remembered the horror he'd inflicted on Centauri POWs after receiving a new batch all too well. Their screams still haunted him.

He'd developed his own method of stimulating a human's nervous system at any point and at any threshold he saw fit. And while it had taken time studying Kione's unique anatomy, he now felt he had a good handle on how to use the same technique on him.

He frowned, watching his assistants strap the alien down through the observation screen on what had become known as the 'bed of hell.' He didn't want to subject Kione to it but he'd run out of options. Drug therapy and other less invasive methods hadn't come close to bringing his mental abilities to the fore. He'd hoped with what was originally designed as torture would provide the result he needed.

Charles pushed in the intercom on the console before him. "Is he ready?"

His assistants nodded and walked out from the laboratory, joining him in the observation room.

"Can you hear me?" Charles asked Kione, who simply stared at the ceiling. The effects of what drugs he'd been given would have worn off by now, so he was obviously ignoring him.

"Okay, listen, Kione, in the hope I can stimulate your nervous system, I'm—"

"Just do what you have to do, Whitlowe," Kione interrupted him, not breaking his gaze into nothingness.

Charles nodded to Le Favre, and she wound the dial at the presets agreed to. "Level one."

Kione's body stiffened at the power running through him, but no change appeared on the readings.

"Go to level two."

The hum of the machine got louder. Kione's eyes closed, and his jaw clenched. It was the first sign of pain. But his brain functions didn't alter.

On to level three they proceeded. Then four. And then five.

Kione convulsed, pounding against his restraints.

Sweat dripped down Charles's brow. He wiped it away and studied the data. The alien's nervous system had been bombarded to within an inch of its life. On the monitor, it looked like a brightly lit-up Christmas tree.

He scowled. "Push it to level six."

"But, Doctor, if we go any higher, it'll kill him," Le Favre warned.

"Just do it!"

She sighed and turned the controls. Kione finally gave in and shrieked out in agony.

Ceres

The transport pod they'd taken to Ceres wouldn't have been Jason's first choice, but the vessel from Mars was an excellent cover for himself, Agent Moss, and the ten other Intel operatives.

Disguised as FIFO workers, in the green coveralls of the Reo Mining Company, they left the dank and smelly ship behind and made their way to their allotted barracks inside the small mining settlement. For somewhere so close to the civilization of Earth, it was a rough part of the universe.

After cleaning themselves up with a shower, or at least the Ceres equivalent, Jason and Moss proceeded to the local tavern. It was a grungy cesspit, reminding Jason too much of his old haunt on Odyssey Station. They took a seat at a booth, and the Intel agent promptly ordered two Ceres Delights from a waitress.

"Ceres Delights don't come cheap here." The bar's publican came over to see them especially. "It'll cost more than you're worth."

"That's okay. Perhaps we'll have a beer then," Moss said. "And after, you could show us the back room. I hear you have quite the taxidermy collection."

Jason turned up his nose.

The barman gestured toward a door near the bar. "Why don't you come and see now."

Moss stood and told Jason to follow him. When they entered the back room, the publican flicked on the lights, bathing it in dull illumination. It was relatively spartan apart from a few covered-up pool tables. However, sure enough, on the walls were the stuffed animal trophies.

The publican closed the door behind them and shook Moss's hand. "I'm Agent Hightower, Ceres station. Good to meet you."

Moss introduced himself and pointed to Jason. "This is Commander Cassidy, CDF. He's coming along for the ride."

Jason chuckled. What he'd witnessed was an act to ensure they were all working for the same team. He shook Hightower's hand. "I thought this stuff just happened in old spy movies."

"We like to keep things simple," the rough-around-the-edges undercover operative told him.

"I guess you can't go wrong with the classics."

Hightower ushered them over to one of the pool tables. He pulled the dusty old cover from it and pressed a concealed button beneath. The slate of the table flipped end over end and revealed a workstation with several components.

"I've received your reports on the kidnapping of the three individuals." He activated the console, and a holographic projection of the casino's blueprints appeared.

"As we've discussed, there's little doubt Trentham's holding them near the central safe."

"Yes, we've read over all the data you sent us." Moss nodded. "Now it's a matter of getting in there and taking out the obstacles."

Hightower waved his hand over the hologram, and several dozen red dots appeared throughout. "These are locations of the armed guards we expect to come up against on the lower levels of the casino."

"Expect to come up against?" Jason looked over the hologram with concern. "So, you can't be absolutely sure?"

"Not to a one hundred percent certainty."

"If any part of this plan fails, my people in there are likely to die."

"That's the risk we run."

"You wouldn't be so blasé if it were your friends down there." Jason stepped toward him, and Hightower puffed out his chest.

"Gentlemen, remember why we're here." Moss separated the pair. "Agent Hightower, can you show us your plan?"

Hightower scowled and returned to the subject at hand. "The first team will go in disguised as casino workers. They'll take out every key guard on the main floor. When they're done, I'll tap into the security systems, giving us access to all points leading to the underground levels. I'll also knock out the lighting and alarms."

He pointed at three green circles on the hologram.

"I'll open the doors here, here, and here. Three teams will go in, eliminate the opposition, and converge at the central safe."

Jason didn't want to admit it, but even with the risk involved, it was a sound plan. By the time anyone knew what was going on, they'd already be at their target.

Moss turned to Jason for his okay, and he nodded. "Good. What's our extraction plan?"

"I've got two pods," Hightower said. "Once the mission's complete, we'll evacuate from the rear entrance, and if need be, the side entrance on the ceiling."

"Okay, let's brief our teams. We get this done at twenty-one hundred tonight."

Holding Cell

"I'm really getting sick of being locked up."

Aly ran her hand over every part of the wall she could find. It had been the umpteenth time she'd tried to uncover an escape route from their detention. Unlike Darius Lok's makeshift brig aboard *The Thor's Hammer*, there was no clear way out. Her new captors made him seem like an amateur.

"Why don't you sit down and have something to eat?" her father said from the floor in the corner. He offered her the food in his bowl.

She turned up her nose. "I've never had a meal as bad as that grub. Even when times were tough on the *Argo,* we never ate like this."

"Perhaps not, but it's better than nothing. We can't

afford to waste away in here. When Jason comes to find us—"

"Do you think he's coming?"

Althaus awakened in the other corner and slowly opened his eyes. "He probably doesn't even know we're alive."

"A cargo ship doesn't go missing without questions," her dad said. "If Jason knows of our disappearance, which he will, he'll locate us."

Aly wasn't sure whether her father was saying it just for her sake, but regardless, hoped he was right. She couldn't stand another minute being in confinement. She wanted to go home to the *Argo*.

That's if she hasn't been destroyed.

Her dad looked up at her. "What's wrong?"

She sat on the floor beside him. "I've played out what happened over and over since they threw us in here. I can't seem to get my head around how easily they took us by surprise when we were returning to Ganymede Station."

"We saw Trentham's ship approaching on the scanners."

"Right. But before we knew it, they boarded. There was no other vessel on our screens."

"It was a chaotic time." Her dad shrugged. "The *Argo's* systems were shot from rescuing you at Io. Our scanners could've been playing up."

Aly pondered, no closer to an explanation. He waved the bowl of food in her face again, and she relented, taking a piece of whatever was inside it.

FORTY-ONE

Tokyo, Earth

"Doctor Tai, you have an incoming message."

Susan opened her eyes ever so slowly at the computer's alert. Without thinking, she tried to place her feet on the floor. But they didn't move.

While the nightmares had subsided since her initial surgery on Outpost Watchtower, she'd still not gotten used to waking without the use of her legs.

Her wheelchair had crept away from the sofa and sat in the middle of the living area. Assuming she left the brake off, she threw herself to the floor and crawled with her arms like a soldier through the muck. If there was one thing Susan took out of her disability, it was that her upper body was the strongest it'd ever been.

"Doctor Tai, you have an incoming message," the computer repeated.

"Just wait!"

Susan grabbed her chair and hauled herself up. She

waved her messy hair aside and turned to the wall monitor. "Open commlink."

The blank screen was replaced with the image of an ageing man with thin wisps of gray hair. Behind him was the vast cityscape of Lexington, Centauri's capital city.

"Doctor Tai," he greeted her with a smile. *"My apologies for not being able to contact you sooner."*

"No need to say sorry, Mister Buehner, it's I who should have thought about the differing time zones."

"What can I do for you. Doctor?"

"May I first ask if this is a secure channel on your end?"

Buehner ran his hands over his workstation. *"It is now."*

"Thank you," Susan said. "I've been in contact with several people on Earth and Centauri regarding a man who may have committed war crimes while in the commonwealth government's service. So far I've found little information."

"Well, if there's anyone who can help, it's me. I have a large array of records dating from the outbreak of hostilities all the way to the final surrender. With that said, you should understand at the conflict's conclusion, investigations on both sides determined few violations took place at the hands of Earth forces."

"Yes, well, history is written by the victors," Susan lamented.

"And those victors tend to dispose of proof painting them in a bad light."

"Let's hope your archive is as extensive as you claim." She reached down and pressed the panel on the coffee table. The file photo of Doctor Whitlowe appeared on the monitor.

Buehner froze, and his mouth quivered.

Tai raised an eyebrow. "Do you recognize this man?"

"Not personally, but his features..."

"I've determined he was an extractions officer for Earth Intel. He went by the name of William Ramsey. If there's anything you can tell me..."

"Leave this with me, Doctor. If I gather any concrete information, I'll let you know."

The screen when blank, and she let herself feel some hope. Kione felt closer than ever.

But will it be too late?

Ceres

"We're going in now!"

The initial obstacles were out of the way, and Hightower and his team eliminated the guards on the main casino floor with ease.

Jason had a communications device fixed over his ear, and through it he listened in to Hightower make his way to the security section. Several shots echoed over the commlink, followed by silence.

"We're in!" came the call. *"All teams stand by."*

Jason gripped his rifle and glanced at Agent Moss

and the other two operatives by the side entrance. It seemed like an eternity waiting for the order.

"*Security system compromised,*" Hightower wailed. "*All teams, go!*"

The door clicked open, and Jason pulled his infrared visor over his face. Moss stormed through and immediately dispatched their first victim at the top of the stairwell with a knife through the man's face. Jason grabbed the goon before he fell over the railing and placed him on the floor. Moss pointed downward, and they all followed.

Two more guards appeared from the darkness at the bottom of the stairwell. The frenzy of the situation had them confused. Moss crept up behind one and slit his throat while one of the other operatives cracked the butt of his rifle into the back of the other's head.

They continued onward through the corridor, turning left and then right. Jason had already committed the map to memory and realized they were only fifty meters away from the central safe room.

Around another corner, bullets rained on them from ahead. Moss lurched backward and fell to the floor in agony. "Damn it!"

Jason pulled him behind cover to safety and inspected the bloody wound to his arm.

"They're not supposed to be there!" Moss managed to say.

"A hiccup, no doubt." Jason turned to the other two operatives and pointed back down the corridor.

They jumped out from each side and fired. Their

assailants then collapsed in a heap with bullets to the chest.

"Can you keep going?" Jason asked Moss.

The Intel boss heaved himself up and grabbed at his rifle. "This won't stop me." He led them forward while reports came in from other teams over the comms. They'd all hit resistance but were still on track.

Jason got to the last corner and peeked around it. At the end was the large safe door.

"There's no one standing guard." Jason narrowed his eyes. "This is too easy."

Moss propped himself up with Jason's shoulder and peered at their target. "My arm says differently."

They carefully moved down the corridor and reached the locked door. The other two teams arrived from the adjoining corridors, and within minutes they hooked up the explosives. Everyone stood back, and the seemingly immovable locking mechanism fell to the floor with a clang.

Jason was the first on the scene and used all his strength to pull the door open. Inside was just as dark as the outside. But three figures stood out. He reached for the lights and flicked them on.

Aly, Kevin, and Althaus all turned toward him.

Relief overcame Jason, and he hurried to Aly to put his arms around her. But they didn't find anything solid. His arms wrapped around nothingness, as if she weren't even there.

"Holograms!" Moss yelled from the doorway.

Jason gazed at Aly's blank expression, and her hologram disappeared into oblivion along with the other two men.

"Mister Cassidy, I am disappointed."

Jason and all the operatives clenched their weapons at the female voice echoing around them. It was the same one he'd heard on the *Argo* when it was docked at Ganymede Station. "Ravi Trentham..."

"Here I was hoping we could do business with each other. Instead, you went behind my back. You failed the test."

Jason peered up at a camera and speaker in the center of the ceiling. "Failed the test? These holograms... You set this up!"

"I had to see how trustworthy you'd be. Much to my chagrin, I've discovered not very."

"Joke's on you, Trentham. Now we know about all of this, the authorities will shut down every single one of your operations. They'll hunt you down and throw you in prison for life."

She laughed. *"Mister Cassidy, in the corner you'll see a box. Go over to it."*

Jason sighted it and walked toward it with Agent Moss by his side who gave him a wary look.

"Open it," she instructed him.

He placed his hand on each end and opened the lid. The smell was nauseating.

A severed head?

The pair jumped back and waved at the odor emanating from it.

The very dead eyes of Ravi Trentham's decapitated skull stared up at them.

"So, you're not Ravi Trentham." Jason tried to piece the puzzle together. "She was a pawn just like Darius Lok."

"I prefer to see them as expendable resources. Once they're done serving their purpose, I dispose of them."

"Is that what you'll do to my friends?"

"That's up to you, Mister Cassidy. I'm willing to give you a second chance, but to show you how seriously I take this, I'll make a demonstration."

The hologram came back to life and Aly appeared with two obscured guards on either side of her. She had a fearful look in her eyes as another figure approached. In his hand was a large butcher's power saw.

It hummed to life.

"Please, no! No!" Aly screeched.

"You bastards!" Althaus yelled.

"Cut mine off instead!" Kevin wailed.

The saw slashed downward and took Aly's hand clean off. Her scream was unlike anything Jason had ever heard.

"I hope this proves how serious I am, Mister Cassidy."

The hologram disappeared, and Jason fell to the floor, wanting to vomit. "You bitch!"

"I want Kione. Mister Cassidy. The clock is ticking."

The speakers went dead, and Moss grabbed at his wound, pulling Jason to his feet. "Let's get out of here, Cassidy."

FORTY-TWO

UECS Sabre

"Agent Moss is out of surgery."

Jason glanced at Captain Shila as she entered the briefing room. "Sorry? What?"

He returned his attention to the viewport and her reflection stared at him while transport pods whizzed back and forth between the fleet and Alpha Station in preparation for the war games.

"Agent Moss." She approached him. "They pulled the slug from his shoulder. He's going to make a full recovery."

"That's good to hear." He closed his eyes and relived the horror of Aly's hand separating from her wrist. The sound of the saw echoed inside his head.

The door opened once again and Admiral Foster appeared. "It's good to see you made it back unscathed, Commander."

"Unfortunately, the mission was far from successful, sir," Jason said.

Foster stepped between them. "I read over the report. It seems you were led down the beaten track."

"The real worry is the anonymity of who we're dealing with. Trentham was one of the smartest criminals of her day with resources to match. Whoever's behind this is in another league."

"Intel agrees."

"Could we be looking at a new player on the scene?" Shila pondered.

"That appears most likely."

"If that's the case, we have to smoke them out of their hole."

The admiral took a seat at the head of the table. "The plan's being formulated as we speak." He eyed Jason with caution. "When the time comes to rendezvous with them at the coordinates, we'll hit them hard."

Jason raised an eyebrow. "Destroy or capture?"

"If possible, neutralize and board their vessel, otherwise—"

"Hold on a minute. Have we learned nothing from Ceres? If we go in all guns blazing, more than Aly's hand will be lost this time." Jason sat in the seat beside Foster. "Let me have Kione—"

"That's out of the question. The Ministry of Defense have made it clear they won't give Kione up."

"I wouldn't hand him over."

"What would you do?"

"Something akin to fishing."

"You'd use him as bait? That's a risk they're not willing to take. Kione is far too valuable." Foster's expression softened. "Look, I completely understand the situation you're in. This new group we're facing... It's disturbing to say the least."

"No, Admiral." Jason waggled his finger at him. "You know what's disturbing? Seeing a person you grew up with have her hand chopped off right in front of your eyes with no way to stop it." He stood, nearly throwing the chair to the floor. "My friends put their lives on the line for the commonwealth to destroy that sphere, and now when they need help, our government's solution is their probable death!"

Captain Shila approached him. "Commander."

Jason pointed downward at Foster, almost prodding him in the chest. "You're better than this, Admiral. You of all people are better than this." He stared at his uniform in disgust. "Perhaps you should return to the academy. I think your head's gone numb from sitting behind your desk."

"That's enough, Commander!" Shila put a hand on his arm to pull him from the situation.

Jason turned away and headed back to the viewport. Foster and Shila shared a few quiet words, and the Admiral left, leaving Jason to stew.

"You were unfair with Foster," Shila said.

"I know." Jason frowned. "If anyone tried to drum sense into Mueller it was likely him. No one represents the uniform with more honor."

The question is, can I do the same?

Tokyo, Earth

The sun bathed the city in brightness. But a gusty breeze was making it much too cool for Jason's liking. In the distance, Professor Petit sat on a park bench while Doctor Tai had placed her mobility chair beside him. Jason darted and weaved between the several morning runners and took a seat between them in the beautiful Tokyo commons.

"I got your message," he informed them, "and the file you have on this Ramsey guy. He sounds like a real ass."

"That's one way of describing him," Tai said. "What news do you have on the other front?"

"Foster told me the Ministry of Defense's mind is made up. Kione won't be going anywhere, and Command have approved to launch a sneak attack on the ship at the time and coordinates I've given them."

Petit gazed into the distance. "Just when you think things are looking up..."

Jason cocked his head. "What do you mean?"

"Doctor Tai's in the process of collecting statements from survivors on Centauri regarding Ramsey's war crimes."

"Once they're together," she continued, "we can release them to the public. Not only will we get Kione back, but it'll also put a massive dent in Jarret's reputation."

Jason shot up from his seat and the pair looked at him as if he were crazy. "How long until you receive those statements?" he asked Tai.

She shrugged. "By the end of the day hopefully."

"And no one else knows about the investigations?"

"Only the archivist on Centauri. We're keeping it under wraps until he collects all the evidence."

Jason smiled.

"What are you concocting inside that mind of yours, Mister Cassidy?" Petit asked.

"A way to get our people back." Jason sat back down. "Professor, the Seeker weapons and armor we brought from Psi-Aion, that were confiscated by the *Repulse*. Where are they now?"

"In the special development laboratory at TIAS. They're dismantling them to figure out what makes them tick. And if they're possible to replicate."

"Can you get me a suit of armor and a rifle? Preferably one intact."

"It won't be easy, but I should be able to pull a few strings with my colleagues down there."

"Good. There's something else I need that might not be as easy."

"What's that?"

"I need Nora."

Petit's eyes lit up. "Uh, you're right. That'll be considerably more difficult."

"What do you want with the trans-space device?" Tai asked.

"To get Kione out and rescue the others I'll need to

use every trick in my playbook, plus a few more." He turned back to Petit. "What I ask of you will get us in a lot of trouble. My career in the service will be over... again. And I can't imagine either of you could return to the Institute."

"More than likely they'll hang, draw, and quarter us." Petit rubbed his forehead.

"I can't ask either of you to do this, but—"

"I'm in," they both said in unison.

Jason smiled. Just like that, they were about to put their careers on the line and most likely their lives. He'd have to make sure his plan worked. He didn't want to fail them as well.

"Okay, this is what we'll need to do..."

FORTY-THREE

Edinburgh, Earth

The journalist's limousine arrived at the door of the compound and came to a stop. Charles put his hands behind his back and eyed her stepping out of the car from the empty room on the top level of the facility. He closed his eyes. His work had taken it out of him, and he'd been dreading this meeting more than most. This particular reporter came with a reputation as a tough nut to crack. He'd have to use every piece of his charm to keep her at bay.

One of Charles's assistants greeted her at the door and ushered her into the building. Before he knew it, she'd brought his guest up the stairs.

"Doctor Whitlowe, Miss Caldwell's here to see you," his assistant said.

Charles smiled and shook Caldwell's hand. "A pleasure, Miss Caldwell. Welcome to Scotland." He gestured to a table, and they took a seat opposite each other.

"Thank you for allowing me to come here, Doctor Whitlowe."

He looked knowingly at her. "You gave me little choice. No one is supposed to be aware of my activities here. I assume you came into that knowledge by my predecessor, Doctor Tai."

Caldwell didn't answer.

"I'll take that as a yes." He tapped his fingers on the table. "I suppose she hasn't been able to let go of the past."

"That I can't say. But if I were to guess, I'd say she's concerned for Kione's wellbeing."

"I gave her a tour of this facility to allay any of her fears." Charles frowned. "It seems she's taken advantage of my gentle nature."

Miss Caldwell studied him and smiled. "Perhaps it was women's intuition on her part."

"What does your intuition tell you?"

"Well, I'm not sure yet. Hopefully by the end of my time here I'll have a better idea."

"Hmm." Charles went to tap his fingers on the table again but stopped himself. He wouldn't show her any twitches that might make him appear weak. "What brings you here today?"

"I'm here to ask you some questions about your program."

"That'll be very difficult, considering it's a classified project. You shouldn't know about it, and I shouldn't be here entertaining such a conversation."

"Then why am I here?"

"You claim you have information on my past," he sighed. "I saw what you did with the Orion V story. You're beholden to your own rules. I've got no doubt you'd release what you know whether it's true or not. I guess I allowed you here to ensure you left with the truth."

The guard at front of the facility lit up a cigarette and turned his back to the limousine.

Jason stepped out of the driver's-side door, seeing his opportunity. He slowly ambled up behind him and tapped him on the shoulder. "Hey, you got a light?"

The man spun around and beheld Jason in all his glory, kitted out from head to toe in Seeker armor, helmet and all. The guard stumbled backward in shock and grabbed at his sidearm.

Jason didn't give him a second more to react and chopped at his throat, cutting off his air. He dragged the guard up the stairs to the front door and pressed his thumb against the panel.

It opened.

"Thanks." Jason threw the goon aside and entered to another unsuspecting pair of victims.

"Hey, you have to stay outside and keep an eye on —" the older of the two said before his mouth dropped.

Jason pulled out his sidearm and fired, sending him sprawling to the floor. The Seeker weapon was on the non-lethal setting, but it still packed a punch.

The second guard tried to raise his rifle, but Jason swatted it away and punched him in the face, knocking him out cold.

Marissa handed Whitlowe a large data tablet from her bag. "In the last few days, several statements have been collected from witnesses claiming you were involved in atrocities during and after the war. Primarily on Centauri military personnel and civilians."

He perused over all the documents Tai had received from the archivist on Centauri and passed it back to her. "It seems you've got me confused with someone else. These people speak of an extractions officer by the name of William Ramsey."

Marissa removed another tablet from her bag and clattered it across to him. It was his sealed records with photo evidence proving he was the same man. He glanced down at it, and she could swear the blood from his face drained.

"How could you have found all of this?"

Jason prowled down the corridor and entered the elevator. With the plans Tai had given him, he sent the car downward. When the doors parted, another guard appeared. Jason decided not to be so cocky this time, instead pointing and firing straight away.

Out if the corner of his eye, a shadow flashed past. He turned. It was one of Whitlowe's staff in a white lab coat. He locked eyes with Jason and rushed off down the corridor. Jason bounded after him and rounded a corner where he found the lab technician heading toward a wall panel to alert security to his presence. He dived on him just before he reached it. Jason grabbed him by the head and drove his knee into his back.

"Where's Kione!" he demanded.

The scrawny man struggled to break free. Jason pushed his face into the floor and broke his nose. Blood gushed out and poured over the white tiles.

"I won't ask a second time!"

"He's on the habitat level. Two levels down," the man finally relented.

"Thank you." Jason rolled him over and punched him in the head, knocking him unconscious.

He then got up and made his way back into the other corridor. Deciding against the elevator, he took the stairwell instead, barreling down the steps toward the bottom. The corridor was clear and he hurried down it, checking several empty rooms. Around the corner at the end, four guards stood in front of one door in particular.

Bull's-eye.

The element of surprise would be difficult, but Jason had planned for that. He hadn't asked Professor Petit for the Seeker armor for nothing. He took a deep breath in and gripped his sidearm. He stepped out into the corridor and fired at the first guard he saw. His target fell quickly.

The others spotted him and commenced unloading their arsenals. A barrage of bullets rained toward Jason from their heavy-duty rifles. The pressure of the projectiles against his armor created a bizarre sensation. It was like the pitter-patter of rain on a tin roof. He marveled at the technology. If it weren't for the black suit, he'd have been ripped to pieces.

He fired at the next guard. The shock setting of his weapon sent them scattering while the other one closest to him tried to play the hero and charge at him with the butt of his rifle. With the ease of the suit's movement he'd gotten accustomed to on Psi-Aion, Jason shuffled aside and threw the man to the floor. With a single pull of the trigger, he put him down.

The last holdout stood in front of the door and emptied every bullet he had left into Jason's chest. He slowly walked up to the henchman and reached for his rifle. The man dropped it and stared at Jason like a deer in the headlights. The edge of his mouth quivered, and he put his hands in the air.

Jason raised his sidearm and shot him. He kicked the prone body aside and pressed the panel near the door, but it was locked. He adjusted his gun to its highest setting and fired.

It blew a hole in the bulkhead the size of a football, and the door slid open. He hurried through the haze of shrapnel in the air and found Kione lying on a bed surrounded by medical scanners.

"Kione!"

The alien didn't respond.

Jason removed his helmet and slapped his unconscious face. "Kione!"

"Jason Cassidy?" Kione stirred.

Jason took his shackles off. "Are you with us in the land of the living?"

"Barely." Kione's eyes opened, and he hauled himself upright. "We've got to stop meeting like this."

"You've got to stop getting yourself in so much trouble." Jason helped him from the bed. "Can you walk?"

Kione planted his very wobbly feet on the floor. "I'll be fine."

"Let's get out of here then."

Marissa did everything she could to keep the smug satisfaction from her face. While she wasn't one of those reporters who enjoyed gotcha moments, this was different. She'd read all the statements on this guy, and if there was anyone who deserved what was coming to him, it was Whitlowe.

The doctor put the data tablet down and stared across at her. "You realize if this gets out, there could be serious ramifications for you."

"Is that a threat, Doctor Whitlowe? Or should I say Mister Ramsey?"

The door creaked open behind him, and Jason entered with Kione at his side with his gun raised. "Stand up, Marissa."

She did so carefully and stood back from the table.

"You, too, Ramsey. Put your hands where I can see them."

Whitlowe did as instructed. "Your partner in crime, Miss Caldwell?"

"The only criminal here is you." Jason stepped toward him, but Kione beat him to it.

He stared at the man with a fury so hostile, Marissa was afraid of what might happen.

Kione put out an open hand. "Your gun, Mister Cassidy."

Jason hesitated before checking his sidearm and handing it to him. Kione looked at the gun and altered the settings back and forth a few times.

Sweat beaded down Whitlowe's forehead. "Kione, I—"

He fired point blank into his stomach, and the doctor launched across the room into a heap. Kione gave the gun back to Jason and stumbled out of the room.

Marissa walked up beside Jason. "Did he kill—?"

"No." He showed her the setting. "He just shocked him."

She breathed a sigh of relief, though wondered if justice would've been better served if he'd killed him instead.

FORTY-FOUR

Cargo Ship Argo

The ride back to the *Argo* was the easiest part of the mission. Jason had left the cargo ship in a geostationary orbit above Scotland with Doctor Tai at the controls, remembering she was a qualified pilot.

On the *Julieanne's* arrival, Jason ever so gently helped Kione through the airlock into Tai's capable hands.

"I'm so relieved to see you, Kione." She ran her medical scanner up and down him. "How are you feeling?"

"I've been better." He chuckled. "I want to thank you."

"Thank me?"

"You got my message."

She frowned. "I'm sorry it took so long to come and get you."

Marissa came out of the pod, and Tai looked at her in shock. "She's coming with us?"

Jason frowned. "She wanted to see this through."

"I hope you understand what you're getting yourself into if you stay aboard, Miss Caldwell."

Marissa smiled. "A story even bigger than my last."

Jason wondered if he should have just thanked her for her role in rescuing Kione and sent her on her way. However, from their relationship many years earlier, he remembered how stubborn she could be and likely wouldn't have taken no for an answer regardless. He just hoped she was built as tough as he remembered.

"Come on, let's get you to the infirmary," Tai said to Kione.

Jason followed them onto the elevator, with Marissa not far behind him. "Has Professor Petit sent a message yet?"

Tai shook her head. "No."

Jason had hoped to have all his ducks in a row by now. "This'll be tight."

When they came to the top of the elevator shaft, Tai took Kione to the infirmary while Marissa went with Jason to the bridge.

Jason made a beeline for the helm and plugged in their new coordinates. "Next stop: Luna."

Serenity Science Station - Luna

Javier had barely eaten all day. He never ate when he was nervous, and his grumbling stomach was letting him know about it.

He'd noticed how easy it was for people like Jason

Cassidy in these situations. He was trained for it. Javier wasn't. Cambridge hadn't given him the skills.

I'm no secret agent.

It hadn't helped matters organizing a dinner with Doctor Song Ji-min before everything was about to go down. With the Vladivostok Project on hold indefinitely and Nora handed over to him, he'd asked her to join his team. With the Ministry of Defense's blessing, she'd begrudgingly accepted, and Javier had done everything he could to smooth things over with his noted rival.

"You keep checking your watch. Did you make other plans?" she said.

Javier glanced up from his commband across the table at Song apologetically. "I told a friend I'd send them a commlink."

"You double-booked." She crossed her arms sarcastically. "That's unlike you."

"It's Doctor Tai. I guess with everything happening at the moment, I didn't schedule it—"

She smiled. Something Javier wasn't used to. "If you need to go, please don't stay on my account. I've got paperwork back home to look over. And to be fair, the food here isn't that good."

Javier chuckled at her taunt to his mother nation. But even he accepted it was a pretty substandard French restaurant. "Are you sure?"

She nodded. "Go."

"Thank you." Javier jogged off, sicker than he already felt. Even though Song was an adversary, lying to her made him ill. He kept telling himself it was for a good cause.

Back through the facility, he made his way to his lab and opened the door with his thumbprint. The room was bathed in the same darkness he'd left it in when he'd shut up shop earlier in the evening. He flicked the lights on and gazed through the observation screen beyond the bank of computers at his prized possession. "Hello, Nora."

The trans-space actuator as it was now officially known sat on its pedestal at the heart of the laboratory. Little did anyone know that it was soon to be gone for good. He'd filled Jason in on all its intricacies and instructed him how to install it on his ship.

Javier ran his hands over the main console and turned off all the alarm systems. He then activated the scanners by tapping into the station's operations center, and sure enough, the *Argo* was on course and right on time.

He contained his excitement at the fact they must've been successful in rescuing Kione. He tapped his fingers over the adjacent station and initiated a secure commlink. "Petit to *Argo*. Come in."

"This is the Argo. *It's good to hear you, Professor,"* Jason Cassidy said. *"I was getting worried."*

"Everything is under control." Petit again checked the scanners. "Now, once I launch Nora, I'll direct her to your ship's cargo bay. You should be clear of all Luna security patrols."

"Thank you."

"Are you sure you understand everything I've told you about the actuator? She—"

"Piece of cake."

Petit rolled his eyes. "I want to see it and you back in one piece."

"That's the plan." There was a pause on the other end of the channel. *"I hope you realize what this means for you when—"*

"You leave that with me." Javier's stomach grumbled again and he pressed at his console. "Are you ready?"

"Ready."

FORTY-FIVE

Cargo Ship Argo

After everything they'd gone through, the *Argo* reached the coordinates for their rendezvous early. Jason yawned, looking over the scanners.

"Don't fall asleep," Marissa said, entering the hatchway onto the bridge.

"I doubt I'll be sleeping for a while." He frowned.

She approached him and put her hand on the back of his chair, checking over his readings on the operations station. "Any contact yet?"

He shook his head.

"Doesn't that seem strange to you? From everything we've seen so far, I can't imagine they're likely to be tardy."

She was right. Something was up.

But what?

Marissa sat at the helm and stared off into the distance.

"Are you having second thoughts?" Jason asked, noticing her discomfort.

"No." She snapped out of her trancelike state. "Why?"

"I'm not sure. Since coming aboard, you've just seemed different. I can't read you."

"Were you ever able to?"

"I guess not." Jason wondered if that's what attracted him to her the most.

"There is actually something I've got to tell you."

"Oh?"

An alert rang out on his console.

Great timing...

"Someone's opening a commlink." He checked the scanners. "From where, I can't say. The board's clear."

"Mister Cassidy, nice of you to make it on time," the familiar female voice said over the speakers.

Jason peered down at the scanners, once again making sure he wasn't going crazy. "Umm, where are you?"

"Turn around."

Jason furrowed his brow and shooed Marissa from the helm. He fired the *Argo's* maneuvering thrusters and rotated the ship one hundred and eighty degrees. There staring them in the face was a ghost from the past.

He deactivated the commlink. "That's a Centauri vessel."

"How's that possible?" Marissa asked. "All their vessels were destroyed after the war and their defense forces disbanded."

"I'm not sure, but I could pick those ships out of a lineup ten light-years away." Though Jason had never seen one of its design. It was more modern and sleeker than the clunkers they'd used in the war. "What's more worrying is why our scanners can't detect it."

"Stealth technology?"

"It doesn't exist."

"This would seem to prove otherwise."

Jason couldn't argue with that, and he reactivated the commlink.

"Do you have Kione, Mister Cassidy?"

"I do."

"Are you ready for the transfer?"

"I am."

"Good. Standby to come aboard our ship. We'll—"

"If it's all the same to you, the *Argo* will stay right here. You can dock with one of our airlocks. The transfer will take place in our cargo bay."

"Mister Cassidy, we—"

"You've dictated all the terms to this point. Kione's obviously very valuable to you, so in this instance, you'll do as I say." It was the only thing he imagined stopping her from boarding his ship by complete surprise with her stealth tech as she'd no doubt done to Aly and the others in the Jovian system.

Silence greeted him on the other end of the channel.

"I'm waiting," Jason reiterated.

"Very well, Mister Cassidy, the transfer can take place on your ship."

"Oh, and let's keep it civil. No more than one gun."

"One gun it is."

"See you soon." Jason deactivated the commlink. "Now it begins."

Serenity Science Station - Luna

Song hated playing catchup. Ever since the Vladivostok Project had been put on hold and she'd accepted to join Javier's team, she found her evenings bogged down in paperwork, doing everything possible to become an expert on transient space. In between, she also continued her work on the automated defense system for the day her team could return to it.

She placed the last of her data tablets down on her bedside table and threw her head back on her pillow. The ceiling blurred. She'd overdone it, as always. Her mind was so full, she felt like her brain might open a trans-space vortex all on its own. She switched off the lights and closed her eyes. After thirty minutes of trying to get to sleep, she pulled herself up and put on a change of clothes.

Something was gnawing at her about the delivery system on Nora, and she wouldn't be made to look like an idiot by Javier in the morning if she didn't understand it. She left her room and roamed the station's empty corridors until she reached the laboratory. She put her thumbprint on the panel and walked inside.

The lights were out. Song half expected to see Javier there, considering how hard he worked. But instead, the room was empty. She activated the lighting and turned from the banks of computers to make a coffee. After taking a sip, she gathered a data tablet from the desk. When she spun back around, she stopped dead in her tracks. Her coffee cup fell from her hands and shattered all over the floor.

She found the closest intercom and slammed her hand down on it hard. "Professor Ji-Min to Security. Nora is gone!"

UECS Sabre

"Bridge to Captain Shila."

Shila opened her eyes and reached for the intercom, slapping it, not too impressed with being woken. "This better be good."

"It's a commlink from Admiral Foster."

"At this time?" She threw her legs out of bed and made herself presentable by putting on the crinkled uniform jacket she'd worn the day before. "Pipe it through down here."

Foster's face appeared on her wall monitor. He looked as tired as she felt.

"I didn't take you for a night owl, Admiral."

"I'm sorry to wake you, Captain, but we've just received word from the Serenity Station on Luna. Nora's been stolen."

"The trans-space actuator? How—"

"It appears Professor Petit broke in this evening and launched the device without authority."

While she didn't know the professor personally, she couldn't imagine someone of his standing doing such a thing.

An image appeared on the monitor beside Foster. *"Luna Security sent us this."*

A video played of Nora flying away from the moon's surface and entering the rear bay of a small cargo ship. But it wasn't just any cargo ship.

"Cassidy..." She rubbed her temples, wishing it was a surprise.

"This was also given to us from the Ministry of Defense."

Another video appeared of Jason, dressed neck to toe in black armor, with Marissa Caldwell fleeing from a building helping someone into a limousine. The individual looked unlike anyone she'd ever seen before.

"Cassidy broke out with the extraterrestrial known as Kione from a secure scientific facility in Edinburgh not long before his jaunt to Luna," Foster informed her. *"It seems he has every intention of planning to free his crew."*

Shila hardly blamed him. Command had royally stuffed up their handling of the situation telling him to accept that his friends may end up being collateral damage. "It makes little sense, Admiral. We have the coordinates and we have the time of the rendezvous. It's still a day away. We'll catch him before they can make any transfer." Then she realized. "That's if he gave us the right information in the first place..."

The cunning bastard.

"He never gave us the real time and coordinates." She shook her head. "He knew all along Command wouldn't play ball with him."

Foster nodded. "That would be my guess as well."

"What are my orders, Admiral?"

"Set course for the coordinates. If you find Cassidy, seize his ship and bring him in. Kione must be returned at all costs."

"Aye, sir."

The monitor went blank, and her room reverted to darkness. She would have preferred to return to her warm bed but knew she'd need all her wits about her when she caught up with her soon-to-be-ex first officer.

FORTY-SIX

Cargo Ship Argo

An amber light on the panel near the *Maybelle's* airlock flicked on, confirming the seal with the Centauri ship.

Jason clenched his Seeker sidearm with a tight grip, waiting for the walkway between the two ships to pressurize. When the green light appeared, the door promptly opened.

Althaus and Kevin walked onto the *Argo* first. Aly followed not far behind with her hand, or lack thereof, wrapped in a bloody bandage.

The final person through the airlock was a short woman in stature with a large rifle and a determined stare. She and Jason glared at each other like two rivals in an old, one-horse town from the Wild West. All that was missing was the tumbleweed.

"It's good to see you, Mister Cassidy," she said in the same voice he'd come to know since Ganymede Station. "And you brought my prize with you."

Jason glanced at Kione beside him. "That was the agreement, wasn't it?"

"I'm glad we could reach an understanding." She winced and reached for her head.

"Are you okay?" he asked Aly.

She nodded weakly, but her face was as white as a ghost.

The woman stepped closer to Jason while keeping her gun trained on her captured trio. "Enough talk. Let's do the exchange."

"I—"

"She won't let you go," Kione said, cutting Jason off. "She plans to do the transfer and destroy the *Argo* when they detach."

"How—" The woman rubbed the bridge of her nose in pain, and blood spilled out from one of her nostrils.

Jason put a hand on Kione's shoulder. "You're reading her mind?"

"Somehow, Whitlowe awakened my abilities. Not that he knew it. I made him believe he'd failed, so he'd think I was worthless to him."

"You went through all that pain for—"

Kione nodded.

The woman grabbed at her nose again, but more blood seeped out.

"Her name's Jennifer Costas," Kione continued. "She's a former fighter of the Centauri Rebellion and a member of a new underground. Their aim is their planet's independence and Earth's annihilation. They want me, hoping to create a super soldier."

"Seems you're a man in demand, Kione."

Costas's legs wobbled beneath her. Whatever Kione was doing wasn't part of the plan, but Jason figured he could use all the help he could get.

He brought his commband close to his face. "Do it, Doctor."

From the airlock, a clang sounded followed by a clunk. The two vessels parted from each other, and Costas spun around. Her eyes bore into Jason's like daggers. "What have you done!"

"You started this game, Miss Costas." He smirked. "I was never going to let you just stroll in here and take Kione. His days of rotting in basements are over."

"What do you think you're playing at?" She raised her weapon at him. "Your ship is no match for mine."

Susan buckled herself in at the helm and the stars drifted as Jason broke the seal to the Centauri ship. She wasted no time doing as Jason had asked and rotated the *Argo* toward the ominous Centauri ship, punching the thrusters and slamming the *Argo* into reverse. With a flick of her wrist, she activated the trans-space actuator.

"I hope this works." She glanced at Marissa, sitting at the operations station.

The Centauri ship quickly altered course and pursued. Susan double-checked her console, confirming the actuator had been switched on.

A majestic light show of swirling reds and purples

appeared in all its splendor between the two ships. It grew from the size of a dinner plate to the size of a fleet cruiser. The Centauri ship veered sharply to port and fought against the harsh forces of the trans-space anomaly.

But their fight was in vain. It tumbled from its axis and the vortex grabbed hold of her, pulling the vessel in, disappearing as if it hadn't even been there.

Susan brought the *Argo* to a standstill and corrected its course. She pressed in the intercom. "Tai to Cassidy. Mission accomplished up here."

"Thank you, Doctor. Good work."

Jason deactivated his commband. "Seems your ship's gone."

Costas tightened her grip on her rifle. "What did you do with it?"

"It's somewhere out near Pluto, I think. I can't remember exactly." He shrugged. "Now would be a good time to put your gun down."

Costas darted her eyes around. "You fought us during the war, Cassidy. You know we don't give up."

"I also recall your leaders were so consumed by hate to achieve their goals they lost their humanity in the process. It not only brought them down but killed millions of your people. It put your cause behind for decades."

"You Earth types are so naïve. We do what we have

to for our sovereignty. The commonwealth will never let us be truly independent unless we take it..." She trained her gun on Kione. "And if we can't have the secret to Kione's DNA, then neither can you."

Jason pulled his sidearm upward to beat her trigger finger, but instead she collapsed to the deck, and her rifle dropped to her feet. She screamed out in distress and grabbed at her head in agony. Althaus hurried to her side and kicked her weapon across the deck. Costas curled up in a ball a cried out one final time before gurgling and falling silent.

Kevin kneeled down and took her pulse. "She's dead."

Kione's mouth quivered like an innocent three-year-old who'd just stomped on an ant hill. "I didn't mean to kill her."

Jason went to say something, but Tai cut him off over the intercom.

"I hope you've got everything under control down there. Because we have company up here."

Waiting for them on the bridge was the image of the *UECS Sabre* fast approaching. Jason chuckled ironically, knowing in his heart of hearts it would be Captain Shila sent to bring him in.

Althaus proceeded to the systems station while Kevin and Kione tended to Aly at the rear of the bridge, placing a medi-sealer over her hand.

"They're opening a commlink," Althaus said.

Jason sat in the captain's chair, next to Marissa who stood by his side. "Let's hear it."

"Commander Cassidy," Shila said, her voice echoing through the speakers.

"Captain. I should've realized being so close to Earth we'd have the CDF near at hand."

"Cassidy, you've done what you came here to do. Under direct orders from CDF command—"

"You want Kione and you're here to arrest me."

She didn't reply.

"Kione isn't going anywhere," he said to her.

"Think about this, Commander."

"I have, Captain. I know my career in the service is over." He glanced at Kione and Aly. "I can live with that. I want to thank you for believing in me and giving me a second chance. Now I have to do what's right."

He nodded toward the helm. "Do it, Doctor."

Tai ran her hands over the controls, and another trans-space vortex appeared. "Everyone, buckle up."

Jason took a deep breath. "Take us in."

FORTY-SEVEN

Jason opened his eyes and flinched at the darkness surrounding him. He tried to move but couldn't budge.

Where in the hell...?

He tugged at his harness locking him in place and immediately remembered where he was. He pulled at the buckles and released himself from the captain's chair.

"Mister Cassidy?"

Out of the night, Kione appeared like a stalker from an old horror movie.

Jason gingerly staggered toward the rear of the bridge where the alien approached. "I think it's time you started calling me Jason. We've been through too much together for all these formalities."

"Very well. Jason it is."

"How long have you been awake?" he asked.

"Only a few minutes."

Around the bridge, Doctor Tai and Marissa were the next to regain consciousness. Kevin, Althaus, and

Aly soon followed. With Kione's help, Jason activated the lighting and main power systems while everyone else came to their senses.

Kevin approached Jason at the systems station. "Thanks for coming to get us."

"You would've done the same for me."

Kevin smiled and slapped him on the back.

"The question is," Althaus said. "Where are we?"

Jason walked to the front of the bridge and turned to his crew. "When I was figuring out a plan to rescue you, I had to come up with a quick getaway. With Professor Petit's help, I managed to get hold of his trans-space actuator. Doctor Tai and I thought we'd kill two birds with one stone."

Behind him, as if on cue, a star appeared through the viewport in all its glory.

"I set a course for the Horizon Cluster. We're here to bring Tyler and Captain Marquez home."

A MESSAGE FROM ROBERT

There's nothing more I enjoy than building relationships with my readers. You can join my Reader's Club for news on my latest releases, receive exclusive bonus content, get free ebooks, and be the first to know about special deals.

Join today by visiting www.robertcjames.com

Milton Keynes UK
Ingram Content Group UK Ltd.
UKHW012154180124
436278UK00001B/2